Scoring with Santa

USA TODAY Bestselling Author

Renee Rose
Theresa Roemer

For more information contact:
Riverdale Avenue Books
5676 Riverdale Avenue
Riverdale, NY 10471
www.riverdaleavebooks.com

Design by www.formatting4U.com
Cover by Scott Carpenter

Digital ISBN: 9781626017306
Print ISBN 9781626017313

First edition, December 2016
Second Edition October 2025

We hope that you enjoyed Scoring with Santa. Please, let us know what you think by taking the time to leave a review on either Amazon or Goodreads. Reviews and recommendations are the life's blood of the independent author and publisher.

Keep up with all things Riverdale Avenue Books at the link here, where you can find free books, exclusive promo codes and latest news: https://preview.mailerlite.io/preview/1098983/sites/136486432257607665/0kJ9TD

If you are interested in being in our ARC reader/reviewer program, you can sign up here: https://preview.mailerlite.io/preview/1098983/sites/160569605411046909/pvCkb9?fresh=1

Chapter One

If Brandy had a quarter for every time a Phenomenal Physiques' employee called her in to fix something, she'd be Bill Gates rich. Okay, that might be an exaggeration, but that's how it felt. At the moment, she was soothing an irrational client.

"Ms. Johnson, I assure you it is highly unlikely your identity would be stolen from Phenomenal Physiques." She tucked an errant strand of her pale blonde hair behind her ear. No matter how hard she tried to keep it contained in a ponytail, the front wisps always slipped out. "We take personal privacy very seriously. No one has access to your credit card number. Once you sign up, all automatic charges are handled by the credit card processing company, that, of course, guarantees security."

Jane Johnson tightened her already thin lips. If the woman held her neck any more stiffly, Brandy feared her head would snap off. "Well, you never can be too sure these days, especially at Christmas time. My sister-in-law had her identity stolen and it took her eight months to sort out."

Brandy attempted to beam assurance and confidence. "I understand your concerns. That's why

1

we take the utmost caution in handling our personal information."

"My sister-in-law's was stolen from her hairdresser's—"

"Were you going to take the kick boxing class today, Ms. Johnson?" Brandy cut in, hoping to redirect.

Jane glanced over at the wall of windows to Studio A, where Alejandro—Alex—Phenomenal Physiques' gorgeous Latino boxing coach had just started warming up his class. "Oh—yes. Yes, I am." Her eyes kept tracing Alex's sculpted chest and shoulders. "We'll talk more later."

Not if I can help it.

Brandy watched Jane hurry over to the door of Studio A, an eager smile replacing the woman's usual dour expression.

Yes, Alex brought happiness to many women's lives. And men's.

"Thanks for talking her down." Jennie, her front desk manager, screwed up her face in sympathy. "You're so good at that. I'm sorry, she wouldn't leave until she'd talked to you personally."

Brandy stifled a sigh, scanning the club for any other emergencies requiring her attention. Launching the health club at 40 had been the culmination of a lifetime of hard work and dreams.

It also had been the end to her marriage, but that was another story.

Four years later, she stood poised to open three new locations. She wouldn't just own a fitness club, she'd run an entire chain. Of course, that would likely mean three times the headaches, but it would be worth it.

Brandy looked at a particularly large, buff man who was working on the equipment with a tall, black athletic youth. Whoa... she looked closer. Not many men were that tall with shoulders as broad as The Incredible Hulk.

"Is that Rick Morehouse over there?"

Jennie blushed. Actually blushed. Rick Morehouse was said to have that effect on women. As Houston's most eligible bachelor, the drool-worthy former Houston Texan quarterback was the darling of both the press and public. He'd coached the local high school football team to win State five years in a row and regularly made charity appearances. In fact, she'd just booked him to play Santa for Phenomenal Physique's charity event, Fostering Christmas, a gift-giving event for foster kids.

She'd also signed up her own son, Sam, an eighth-grader, for Morehouse's football clinic, which ran for the next few Sundays.

"Yes. He asked for you but you were busy. He needed a place to work with one of his students who can't afford physical therapy."

Brandy's smile faded. "Wait....what?"

Jennie twirled a pen over her fingers and Brandy resisted the urge to snatch it from her to hurry the answer along. "Yeah. He said he needed a place and he understood you're interested in giving back to the community, so he came here."

Well, hell.

"Did he sign any liability waivers or complete any paperwork?" Yes, she used to be married to a lawyer. Liability concerns would forever be ingrained in her.

3

"Uh... no."

"Jennie, you can't just let people come into the club without the proper paperwork. What if something happened while they were here? I'd be liable and—" she sighed and left her drooling office manager to her pen-twirling and strode over to the pair of football players.

"Hi, Mr. Morehouse?"

His head jerked up and he straightened, a friendly smile revealing a row of gleaming white teeth. Yes, Mr. All-American, all right. Not her type.

Yeah, right. That was a total lie. The guy had her panties dampening just from being in sniffing distance. His pheromones alone turned her weak-kneed. It wasn't just the perfectly sculpted chest, or the green eyes that popped against his tanned skin and dark hair. It might be the square jaw with the sexy five o'clock shadow. But no, it was the whole package—the confidence, the charming smile, the way he held his hand out and met her eye with enthusiasm, as if he'd been dying to meet her. "Rick."

Total. Player.

She understood why he made Jennie blush. Hell, she'd be blushing, too, if he wasn't ten years younger than her and way too...perfect. For someone else.

She gripped his calloused palm, admiring the size of his hands. She wondered what he could do with those hands besides throw a football... Nope. *Head in the game, girlfriend.*

"I'm Brandy Love—I believe we've spoken on the phone?"

"Yes, we did." He said it with appreciation, and though his eyes stayed on her face, she suddenly felt acutely aware of her cleavage, as if he had looked at her breasts. Probably because holding his hand had made her nipples hard.

She jerked her fingers away, willing herself not to flush. "Listen, I understand Jennie said it was okay for you to work with your student here, but my liability insurance doesn't cover this sort of thing—." She used an apologetic but firm tone, the one she'd perfected after letting her employees run all over her the first year she owned the club.

"I totally understand," he cut in, the warm smile lighting his face. Unbelievably, he stepped a little closer and she swore she sensed his body heat radiating out, warming her skin. "I'm sorry to spring this on you, but I just found out that Donnie doesn't have insurance to cover rehab, and I really need to get him back to 100% before the playoffs when the college scouts are coming." He canted his head, the green eyes lifting in appeal. "I realize this isn't standard policy, but I'd be happy to have his mom sign any kind of liability waiver you might need to cover your behind." It was cute that he said *behind* instead of *ass*, and she had a sudden awareness of her ass, as if he was trying to keep himself from checking it out.

But that was silly. She couldn't read a guy's intentions that easily. Especially not with her lack of practice, lately.

And yes, her pussy was still wet, a subtle pulsing keeping it in her awareness.

Damn, she bet no woman had ever told him *no* in his life.

She'd have to be the first. Folding her arms across her chest, partly to keep him from seeing her erect nipples, she held firm. "I'm sorry. I'm happy to have you both here, but not until the proper documentation is in place."

He smirked, like he thought she was full of shit. Or was it because he knew her nipples were hard?

Damn, was she blushing?

The youth looked at her with an innocent, easygoing appeal.

Was she really capable of throwing them out?

"I'll bet you're pretty confident you can sweet talk your way into anything, aren't you?"

The corners of his mouth twitched. "Is this about money, because I'm happy to pay for both our memberships. It's just that we only need it for a few weeks and I thought you were interested in supporting the community—"

"I *am* interested in supporting the community." Her voice had gone up a notch. How did she end up being the bitch here? "And no, it's not about the money. It's just about having the proper liability forms signed by all the parties."

Rick stepped closer, rather than drawing away. They probably taught him that in Flirting 101. "I'll tell you what," he said, flashing that heart-stopping smile at her. His voice was deep and resonant and seemed to go right into her body, activating every cell. "I'll fill mine out right now, and I'll have Donnie's mom sign his tonight so that next time we are set up properly."

She put her hands on her hips. "Somehow I don't think you're taking this—*me*," she spluttered. "As seriously as you should."

Obviously she was right because his smile only increased. He cocked a brow. "How serious do you want to take this?"

6

Her tummy fluttered at the innuendo. Her brain stomped its foot. "Rick Morehouse, that flirty act might work with Houston socialites, but it's not going to work with me."

His lips twitched. "I wasn't flirting. I'm just being friendly."

Half of her wanted to kick him in the shin, the other half considered jumping the sexy man. It was hard enough to run a business as a female entrepreneur in a good 'ol boys state without having Coach Handsome throwing her off her game.

A fire burned in his green eyes, lighting her from head to toe. As if he had some mesmerizing power, she realized she really didn't want to tell him no. Her shoulders dropped in defeat. "Fine." She really hoped nobody got hurt today or it would be her ass on the line.

His smile widened. He had sensual lips, and she imagined he must be the most expert kisser in all of Texas. He'd probably already done toothpaste commercials. She should find time to watch more TV.

"But I will need that liability waiver from his mom here by tomorrow—and yours right now."

"Yes, ma'am."

She wanted to wipe that smirk right off his face. Why didn't he take her seriously?

She whirled around, her ponytail flipping in their direction as she stalked off. And ran right into the leg press machine.

"Ow." *Damn*, her shin. That would be a bruise.

"You okay?"

Shut up, Coach Perfect.

"Fine." She rubbed it, hopping on one foot and

trying to walk away at the same time. "You just worry about yourself over there."

She heard the deep rumble of laughter following her out of the room.

* * *

Rick gazed after Brandy as she and her perfect ass sashayed off down the hallway in perfect rhythm with "Jingle Bell Rock," which was playing over the loudspeakers. She had the yoga butt—all sculpted, lifted muscle that her black stretch pants did nothing to hide. A little too tightly wound for his taste. But a fine ass, nonetheless. Mmm, mm. He'd love to squeeze that ass while…

Student. Student. You have a student present. Get a grip, Rick.

He forced himself to turn back to Donnie, who grinned up at him. "I do believe she liked you, Coach."

"Inappropriate, Donnie." He arranged his features to appear stern. "Twenty more reps with the leg press, let's go."

Donnie gripped the handles of the machine and his brows drew down as he pushed the heavy weights out with his quads. The kid had twisted his knee two months back, and while it hadn't seemed that bad of an injury at the time, he still limped after every practice and game. He'd been out when several of the college scouts had visited, so his last shot was at the playoffs, when Rick's buddy Blake Elway from Texas A&M planned to visit.

Rick had talked to the boy's mom about getting him some physical therapy, but she said they had crappy insurance with a huge deductible so she couldn't afford it.

Donnie huffed as he finished the reps, but when he stood up to go to the next machine, he started right back up. "You should ask her out, Coach. She's totally your type."

"Oh really? What is my type?" *Ice princess with a perfect ass.* Yeah. Even if she wasn't his type, he'd change his tastes for her. His body still pulsed from being so close to her.

The cheeky kid grinned. Two dimples crinkled his milk chocolate skin. "She's totally your type."

Conversations with teenagers often drove him batshit. "Yeah, you said that. I really want to hear what *my type* is."

Donnie jerked his thumb in the direction she'd disappeared and made a scoffing sound. "Well, just look at her. She's…" he trailed off, as if not sure it was okay to call a grown-up "hot" in front of his coach. "Um, good-looking. And she's super fit, so that's your type, right?"

Yeah, apart from the uptight vibe, she probably was his type. Tall and long-legged, her body was lean and toned, without looking too bulky. She had perky tits and that scrumptious ass… The blue-eyed blonde thing could be a cliché, but on her it was perfection.

He smiled. "Maybe."

"Plus, she's bossy like you."

He chuckled. "Bossy, huh?" He wasn't going to touch that one. But he supposed Donnie was right. He definitely admired a self-made woman like Brandy. She made the giggling, air-headed 20-something women he usually dated seem like children. She was a real woman. A grown woman who understood who she was and what she wanted. And yeah, he found that damn appealing.

He definitely wanted another chance to flirt. He'd pissed her off this time, but of course that only made the prospect of chasing her all the more appealing.

"You wanna see bossy? I'll give you bossy." He pulled out his stopwatch. "Put your back against that wall and lower to a seated position for three minutes."

Donnie looked cocky for about the first 30 seconds, and then his face turned red and sweat dripped down from his hairline. "How long's it been?" he grunted.

Rick shook his head. "Keep going. Are you breathing? Sounded to me like you're holding your breath."

Donnie gulped and released some air. "How much longer?"

"Two more minutes."

He blew out his breath in a gust. "Are you serious?"

"Come up halfway so the angle of your knees is more like 45 degrees. That's it. Notice how you engage the muscles that stabilize the knees."

Donnie nodded, his brow furrowed in concentration. He'd only just started giving Rick a little shit back this year. Rick'd had him on the varsity team since Donnie was a freshman and the kid pretty much lived and died by what Rick said, so he didn't mind the little bit of back talk now and then.

"Ugh, come on, Coach," he gasped.

He shook his head, unsympathetic. "Not yet. What experience do you have with dating, anyway?"

Donnie grinned. Sweat beaded at his hairline. "I've got a girlfriend."

"Just one?"

Donnie snorted, but apparently didn't have enough breath or energy to respond.

"Why haven't I seen her around?"

"She—doesn't—go—to Houston High," he spit out between ground teeth.

"Ah, the mysterious girlfriend from another school," he teased. "Sure. I bet she's built like a brick house, too."

Donnie laughed and shook his head. "She's real, Coach. She'll be there for playoffs."

"Sure she will."

Rick looked down the hallway and wondered if he'd see the gorgeous Brandy Love again before they left. He suddenly didn't want to leave without her number. Or another chance to flirt. She wasn't married—at least she didn't wear a ring. Yep, he'd checked.

"Three minutes."

Donnie heaved an exhale and pushed himself upright. "That was brutal, Coach."

"We're almost done. Let's see 30 more minutes on the cycle."

"Ah, man," Donnie whined. "Are you serious? I thought we were done."

"No lip. Get peddling." He lifted his chin toward the row of cycles that ran along the window.

From what Rick could see, Phenomenal Physiques had everything you'd want in an upscale gym—top of the line equipment, competent staff and a beautiful facility, which presently was decked out in

11

festive holiday décor. Yes, he admired the hell out of Brandy Love. She was running a great business here.

He climbed on a cycle next to Donnie. He might as well get his own workout in while he was here. No sense in watching the kid pedal for a half an hour. Besides, he had some pent up energy to burn off since his encounter with Ms. Phenomenal Physique herself.

Yeah, he couldn't wait to see her again. Preferably alone, with their clothes off...

* * *

Damn mic.

She adjusted the headset around her face, but the stupid thing kept shorting out as she spoke. Her yoga students all had their heads lifted, craning their necks to watch her for the next instruction, since everything was coming out garbled.

Screw it. Class was almost over, anyway. She pulled the set off and hung it around her neck. With her voice, she talked them through the Savasana pose. "There are some who say this is the hardest pose, even though you're doing nothing but lying on your backs with your eyes closed."

She glanced around the room and started when she saw the hulking, broad-shouldered figure standing in the doorway, observing. His arms were crossed over his barrel chest and his lips curved into an admiring smile.

Her heart picked up speed. What did he want? And no—she wasn't blushing at his obvious interest in watching her teach.

With effort, she returned her focus to her students and said, "It's normal for the mind to resist this deep relaxation. Savasana is an act of conscious surrender. It takes practice and patience to surrender easily."

Don't glance over again. Do not look over.

Too late—she flicked her gaze to his and caught his heated interest. Her libido roared to life, breasts swelling, nipples hardening until the inside of her sports bra scratched the pebbled tips. Unbidden, the image of his head bent to suck one made her rock on her feet.

"Just bring your awareness to your breath," she sang out, hating how unrelaxing it must sound to have her projecting so loudly instead of speaking calmly into her mic. "Notice your contact with the floor... .and thank your body for all its hard work tonight."

She had a great idea of how to thank *her* body and it involved large calloused hands roaming all over her exposed skin. *Whew.* She blew out a shaky breath.

"And when you're ready, roll to one side and come to sit in half-Lotus or Sukhasana."

She wandered to the front of the room and adopted the described pose. With her palms pressed together in front of her heart, she bowed to her class. "Namaste. The divine in me bows to the divine in you."

"Namaste," they repeated after her.

"Thank you, and I look forward to seeing you all tomorrow." She liked to drop that suggestion while they were in a semi-hypnotic state, to keep them programmed to come to class and committed to their well-being.

They filtered out and Rick moved into the room, filling it with his sheer, masculine presence. She noticed more than a few of her students recognized him and sent looks under their lashes or bold smiles as they passed him on their way out.

Aaaand that was why she needed to avoid him. He was totally a player and if word got around they were flirting, it would be the talk of the gym, if not the town. No, no matter how good-looking and charming Rick Morehouse was, she'd better keep her professional distance.

He sauntered over, once more invading her personal space. "Did that stop working?" He reached out and touched the headset around her neck.

A shiver ran down her spine just to have his fingers so close to her skin.

Touch me.

No. No, way, Brandy-Marie. She used her middle name the way her mom did when she was scolding.

"May I help you?" she made her voice ice cold.

He recoiled slightly, but then the affable grin returned.

"Just wanted to make sure you're okay with me being here."

The truth of the matter was that having Rick Morehouse at her gym was a gift. People would become members because they'd see his presence as an endorsement.

She relaxed slightly. "Of course I am. I'm sorry if I came off as bitchy back there—"

Rick held his hands up. "No, no. I totally understand. You need paperwork." He flashed another sexy grin that somehow conveyed how "cute" he thought her desires for paperwork were. He tilted his head, his gaze turning hungry. "Looks like you could teach me a thing or two about flexibility," Coach Sexy drawled.

Oh Jesus. He was coming on to her again. Of course, every cell in her traitorous body perked up at his proximity and the flirty smile plastered her face before her brain had sent the message not to engage. "Did you need help in that area?" she challenged and let her eyes travel down the length of his body in a mock-critical assessment.

Yes, she liked what she saw, not that she planned to let him on to that secret.

He smirked. "I always need help."

How did he manage to sound so convincing? It might be from upper-level charm courses. Flirting 400.

She folded her arms across her chest, which didn't alleviate her jutting nipples, and walked a slow circle around him, surveying his body like a piece of meat. She was tall, but next to him, she was downright petite. She stopped behind him and reached up to grasp his shoulders, drawing them back. "Yes, it looks like you could use a little opening through the chest."

The heat of his body came through his thin T-shirt—a threadbare Texas A&M shirt in a soft dove grey. That's right—it was his alma mater. He'd been a star even back then, taking the team to the national championship.

"My right shoulder doesn't do much, anymore."

Was his voice deeper than normal? She tried to remember what she'd heard about him. He'd had to quit professional ball due to a shoulder injury, hadn't he? Or was it a surgery gone bad?

"Don't worry," she purred. "I'll go easy on you." She'd give him a little taste of his own medicine. She didn't use it often, but there'd been a time when she knew how to flirt, too.

He made a low, growling sound in his throat. "That's not necessary... I like it rough."

15

Her pussy contracted. *Jesus, what was he talking about?*

As if there was any doubt. They were both talking sex here, weren't they?

She slid her hands down his bulging biceps and hooked them on his elbows, pulling back.

He groaned, yeah, actually *groaned* and she doubted it was from the stretch.

"How's that?" Her voice sounded husky.

"Good....really good."

Her pussy contracted again. He had no idea how good it could be. She held him in the pose for another few breaths, then straightened his arms behind him and put his wrists together. "Interlace your fingers, if you can."

It was a struggle for him, but he managed. She walked around the front of him and stepped close enough to feel the heat from his body. She stroked her palms lightly from his breastbone out to his shoulders.

Perfection. If ever a man was stud material, this one fit the bill.

She slid her hands along his trunk, down his sides, stepping close to wrap them around his lower back. With her nails, she scratched his skin over the thin T-shirt lightly. The bulge of his cock pressed against her belly and she longed to take it in her hand and stroke him until...

No.

Bad idea, Brandy-Marie. Very bad idea.

With great effort, she removed her hands from him and stepped back.

Deep breaths, sister. Step away from the sexy coach.

He caught her wrist as she moved out of his

personal space. He had fast reflexes for a guy who had just been struggling to keep his hands interlaced behind his back. "Don't stop," he murmured, flashing that megawatt smile again.

She forced a chuckle. "Hey, I charge a lot for private lessons. That's all you get for a freebie."

He threw his head back and laughed, a deep rumbling sound that warmed her from the top of her head to the tips of her toes. "Well, how can I go about scheduling one of those privates?"

She looked away, stepping toward the door and forcing him to drop her wrist. "Ah, you know, check with the front desk," she said vaguely with a laugh.

"Actually, I was hoping for your number."

"I'm sure you were," she said over her shoulder.

"Really? You're just blowing me off, huh?"

She stopped and pivoted. He sounded dead sincere now, which surprised her. "Wow, yeah. About that... I'm, uh, not exactly dating right now."

Even if I were, I'd stay way the hell away from a player like you.

Her smile wobbled. This shouldn't be so hard.

He shoved his hands in the pockets of his gym shorts, which few men could pull off and still look manly. He nailed it. She realized with a stab of guilt he was trying to hide the bulge of his erection. "Sure, I get it. No problem."

Had she actually hurt his feelings? Impossible. He was a player.

She hadn't meant to be a tease. She ought to be spanked.

By him. Just before he took her hard from behind... *Brandy-Marie!*

17

She jerked her head toward the door. "I'm just... ah... going to take a shower."

He laughed and the tension between them eased. "Yeah, me too—a *cold* one. I'll catch you later."

She tossed him a grateful smile and got her butt out of there before she did something she'd regret. She didn't stop or glance back, not until she was safely inside the women's locker room, where she leaned against the wall and sighed.

Damn. That was close. Too close. She seriously needed to be careful around that man.

* * *

Rick got in his Escalade and started it mindlessly. Well, that's not true. There were thoughts in his head. But they weren't about driving home. No, his brain overflowed with visions of Brandy pressed against him, the light scrape of her fingernails on his back driving him mad, the graceful column of her neck, those full, glossy lips. Yes, the woman could tease. Had she meant to blue-ball him? Little vixen.

He wondered what her story was. Why didn't she date? Or was that just an excuse? Recent break-up? Another man? The idea of another man in the picture made him grind his molars. If there was another man, Rick sure as hell hoped the bastard realized how lucky he was.

He'd like to crack that ice queen facade of hers and tempt the hot-blooded female beneath it. She was just protecting her business, which he had to respect. He respected the hell out of what she'd created there— it was a superb gym.

If Brandy was his woman, he'd make damn sure she felt like a princess every minute of the day. He considered sending her flowers. No—too cheesy for one thing. For another, she said she couldn't date him, so flowers would be entirely inappropriate. And she already thought he was too flirty.

This required something more casual, like showing up with her favorite Starbucks drink. He'd have to pick the brain of the gal at the front desk for the scoop on that.

Wait—he had it! The microphone. She needed technical help. And if there was one thing he was good at, it was electronics. As a bachelor in his 30's, he'd set up more sound systems and televisions than most people had in a lifetime. He would hook her up with new headsets. It was perfect—not too romantic, but something that would genuinely help her out.

Smiling to himself, he punched up the Verizon store on his phone for the address. He'd stop on his way home and pick up everything he needed to hook her up.

Chapter Two

It was her weekly "playdate" with the girls.

Yes, they called it a *playdate.*

They'd started hanging out back when her oldest, Sam, was just a baby attending Gymboree. She'd met a group of like-minded women there and they'd started a weekly playgroup for the babies. Now, 13 years later, her mommy group had become her close-knit friends, still meeting weekly for playdates. Not with their children—they had long since grown apart. No, their playdates were all about cocktails, gossip and moral support.

She scanned the upscale cocktail lounge and spotted her friends in a large circular booth in the corner near a giant silver Christmas tree.

Angelina, gossip columnist for *Houston Magazine,* looked up from the cocktail menu and gave an enthusiastic wave.

She smiled back and crossed the room in her Kate Spade suit and high-heeled Manolos. She always dressed up for their get-together. It was the one day of the week she had the chance to dress in swanky clothes since the rest of the time she lived in work out duds or her casual, around the house jeans and graphic

T-shirt. And yes, she'd heard you weren't supposed to wear graphic tees or Converse after age 30. Screw 'em. She still looked 30, anyway.

"Hi, ladies." She slid into the booth beside Meg, the doctor's wife. Make that, the doctor's soon to be ex-wife. After 15 years of being an over-achieving stay-at-home mom, Meg was looking for an out-of-the-home job because she was considering leaving her husband.

Juliet scooted over to make room. "Hi, girlfriend! What's the news?" Juliet taught creative writing at the University of Houston.

"Ooh, that looks pretty. What are you drinking?" she asked, looking at Meg's fancy cocktail.

"Pomegranate mojito. It's green and red for Christmas."

"I'll have one of those," she said to the efficient cocktail waitress who had magically appeared beside her. "And a menu." She was starving. It was hard to get enough protein with all the exercise she got these days.

"You got it." The cocktail waitress zipped away and Brandy turned to her friends. "So? What's the word, ladies?"

"I'm considering writing erotic fiction," Meg announced.

Brandy exchanged a glance with Juliet. "Really?"

"Yep. They say it's all the rage these days with the Kindle and Nook e-readers on every laptop. Women can read all the smut they want and no one has to see the cover of the books they're reading."

"Truth." Angelina picked up the plastic toothpick with olives from her dirty martini and sunk her teeth into one of the green olives.

21

Brandy laughed. "Is that what's on your Kindle?"

"Oh, yes." Meg grinned wickedly. "A girl needs a little thrill now and again," she trilled in her Southern accent. I like to read those ménage romances. Two men. One woman. *Mm mm.*"

They all laughed.

"Meg, not to stomp on your fluffy feather pillow, but what makes you think you can write books?" Juliet asked. She had been published in a lot of anthologies and for the past four years Juliet had been working on her first novel. Brandy wouldn't be surprised if Meg's sudden interest in writing made Juliet put her defenses up. After all, she had an MFA in creative writing and a lifetime of experience and still hadn't produced her first book.

Uh oh. She braced herself to run interference or redirect the conversation before feelings got hurt, but Meg didn't seem upset.

"Oh, you can stomp on my pillow all you want. It's just my latest idea." Meg flashed a wry grin and stirred her mojito with the slender bar straw. "It seemed better than standing on the corner with a sign."

"Meg, I'm sure the perfect job situation will show up for you, whether that's writing smut or using your talents in another way." Angelina promised with a wink.

They'd all been pushing Meg to find a career because it seemed like her complaints with her marriage stemmed more from boredom now that her kids had turned into teens, rather than anything her husband was or wasn't doing.

"You can always come and work for me," Brandy reminded her. Meg and her obsessive over-functioning would probably make a better office/business manager than Brandy and Jennie combined.

"Yeah, but I don't want to change our relationship. It would affect the whole group dynamic if you were suddenly my boss. Things might get strange, ya know?" Meg swept a manicured hand around the table to include everyone.

"You're probably right. Speaking of weird and relationships, guess who came on to me at the club today?" Yes, she'd been dying to tell her friends.

"Ooh, who?" Meg cooed and friends leaned in, rapt.

"Rick Morehouse."

Angelina gave an exaggerated gasp. "Lucky lady! Did he ask you out?"

The cocktail waitress arrived with her drink and she ordered a Caesar salad with extra chicken.

"Well?" Meg demanded as soon as the cocktail waitress walked away.

"Yep. He asked for my number."

"And—?" Juliet prompted.

"I told him *no way*. The guy is a player. Besides, I'm not dating right now."

Three sets of shoulders around her slumped. "Brandy—really? You gave Rick Morehouse the brush-off?" This was from Angelina.

"Are you nuts?" demanded Juliet.

"May I have his number?" asked Meg with a saucy smile.

"Hell, *I'd* take his number," said the happily-married Juliet. "Kevin's a big fan, maybe he wouldn't mind a little threesome action."

All five of them erupted into laughter, probably

all trying to picture Juliet's very alpha male husband going along with something like that.

"But seriously, Brandy, why did you blow him off?" Angelina looked like she wished she could take notes for her column.

"Ya'll already know—I'm not interested in jumping into another relationship. I'm working on my career."

Juliet rolled her eyes. "Just because your ex never supported you in this, doesn't mean that dating and having a career are mutually exclusive life events."

Justin not supporting her was the understatement of the year. He'd hated what he called her "obsession" with physical fitness. He was such a baby, he resented anything that took her attention away from him, including their two kids. When she'd started seriously bodybuilding, he flipped out, saying she looked too manly, that women weren't meant to be stronger than their husbands. Of course it was his own personal choice to be an out-of-shape flabby pants big shot lawyer.

No, Justin had wanted her at home, like a 1950's wife, waiting to soothe his nerves with a cocktail and a blowjob every night when he arrived. And sometimes that was fun for her, too. But when she had interests outside the home, he couldn't stand it. He didn't like her having a life or identity separate from him.

"I really and truly don't have time for a relationship. I'm about to open three more locations of Phenomenal Physiques and any time I'm not devoting to the business, I owe to my kids. Our weekly playdate, notwithstanding." She flashed a wide, guilty grin.

She wouldn't give up this time with friends for anything. It had been her lifeline—from raising toddlers, to her transition back to work, through her messy divorce and now as a female entrepreneur who was finally making something of herself. Without this group of women sticking by her side, she might have doubted herself so many times along the way.

"One date. One date to report back to us what Houston's hottest bachelor is really all about," Angelina begged.

She rolled her eyes. "You just want fodder for your column."

"Well, ye-ah. And a few photos. The two of you would make a very handsome couple."

"Sorry, girlfriend. Even if I did date him, I wouldn't dish. I don't need my life showing up on your glossy magazine pages!"

Angelina laughed. "Your loss, sugar. You could have free publicity, and a hot, eligible bachelor."

"But really," Meg prompted, "What's he like? Is he totally full of himself?"

The image of his warm, engaging smile flashed in her mind and a tingle ran across her chest, beading her nipples. "No... I didn't get that impression. He might be a player, but he's definitely as sweet as they all say."

"So if he's just a player, play."

Ah, hell. Her panties dampened just at the *idea* of playing with the beautiful muscled hunk. She shook her head emphatically, partly to stop her friends from pushing, partly to tell her raging libido *No*. Firmly.

Not this guy. Not now. Not ever. She had a fitness chain to launch, and two children who needed her attention and love. There was not a "man wanted" sign up anywhere near her heart. Or her body, for that matter.

* * *

Rick pulled up in front of Donnie's house and parked. He'd forgotten to send the liability waiver home with him for his mom to sign, and he wanted to talk with her, anyway. He wasn't sure she understood the importance of the college scouts and Donnie's rehab. If Donnie was at his best when they came, he could get a full ride to an NCAA Division 1 school.

He knocked on the door. Mrs. Fleming opened it, looking harried. A curvy, buxom woman, her hair had a striking streak of grey in the front. He had called to say he'd like to stop by, but she hadn't returned the call and he'd taken the chance of just stopping in.

"Hi, Mrs. Fleming. Did you get my message?"

"I did and I apologize for not calling you back. It's just been one thing after another here."

A girl around ten or 11 peeked her head around Mrs. Fleming, her beaded braids swinging in her face. She must be Donnie's sister.

"Come on in, it's a mess, but—"

"Please, don't stress on my account. I won't take up much of your time. I just need you to sign this waiver for Donnie to work out at Phenomenal Physiques and I wanted to touch base about the college scout who will be coming to watch the playoffs."

"Come in, come in and sit down. Yes, Donnie was telling me something about that. Texas A&M, was it? Will his knee be an issue?"

"Well that's why I wanted to give him a little extra help to rehab it over the next couple of weeks. I'm obviously not a physical therapist, but we're working on basic strengthening and supporting exercises to prevent it from bothering him in the future."

"Can I get you something to drink?"

"No, thank you, I'm fine." He wanted to set the poor woman at ease. That hectic, stretched-too-thin with time and money aura she gave off came too close to home. Like Donnie, a single mom had raised him. He understood how hard it had been for her to be the sole provider and caretaker.

"Mrs. Fleming, I just wanted to make sure you understand how important it will be for Donnie to be at every practice and do his best."

"Is he not working hard enough? Talking on the phone all the time to *that girl* is distracting you!" She put her hands on her hips and shot Donnie an accusatory glance.

"No, no, no. It's not that. On the contrary, Donnie has been going the extra mile every day and I'm proud of his accomplishments. That's what I should have said first." He flashed her his most charming smile. "I just wanted to make sure you're part of the team, that's all."

"Okay, so what do you need from me?"

"Just that form signed and your blessing for Donnie to continue working intensely with me over the next couple of weeks."

Mrs. Fleming finally relaxed. She picked up a pen and scrawled a loopy signature on the proper line. "Here you go. Are you sure I can't get you something to drink? Or eat?"

He took the paper and stood up, smiling when she took an involuntary step back. His size had that effect on most people.

Just not on sexy blonde fitness club owners, thank goodness.

"No thank you, this is all I needed. I won't take up any more of your time. You all have a great evening."

She bustled behind him to show him out. "Good evening Coach Morehouse." She lowered her voice as they got to the door. "Have I told you how much you mean to Donnie? My son lives and breathes on your words. I don't know how to thank you—"

"It's my pleasure." He cut her off before she got too emotional. "I'll see you again, soon." He offered his hand, but she threw her arms around his chest and gave him a quick squeeze, her heavy bosom pressed against his ribs.

"I mean it. Thank you." Her voice sounded choked.

"You're welcome. Good night."

He slipped out the door, flipping his keys in a circle around his finger. This was the whole reason he coached high school instead of college ball, even though he'd been offered positions all over the state. It was why he worked a job that paid a quarter of what he could've made elsewhere. If he'd ever felt like he was living his life's purpose, it was in moments like these.

Strange, he'd never had the urge to share these moments with anyone before, but he found himself thinking about Brandy Love. Would she take him seriously if she knew he really cared about his kids? That he wasn't just a wealthy playboy who liked to flirt with gorgeous blondes?

Chapter Three

The next night, Brandy stepped into her modest three-bedroom house with three bags of groceries. The traditional house was the best she could afford in Bellaire, the upscale Houston neighborhood where she'd lived with Justin before the divorce. She'd wanted to stay in that area to keep her kids in the same school.

Sam, her 13 year-old, looked up from where he was sitting at the kitchen table, doing homework. "Hey mom. You need help with groceries?"

Her heart swelled. There was nothing sweeter than a chivalrous son, in her opinion. Sam had been running to open doors for her since he was four years old and since her divorce, he'd taken on all the "manly" duties that Justin used to do around the house, like mowing the lawn, taking out the garbage, or carrying in the groceries. "Thank you, hon. You're a star."

She set her groceries down on the counter and started unloading them while Sam went out for the rest of them.

"Hi mom." Claire, her 11 year-old appeared from her room. She'd only started leaving the kids at home unsupervised this year and so far they'd proven themselves responsible. They were only home alone for about an hour by the time they got home from their after school activities. Justin had had a fit, but since he couldn't commit to having them on weekdays, he had no room to complain.

"Are you wearing makeup?" she demanded.

Claire blushed. She'd clearly been playing "salon" because her straight blonde hair had been pulled into a one-sided French braid.

"I was just practicing. How does it look?"

It actually looked amazing, but she was so not ready for her tween to grow up. "It looks nice, sweetie, but don't wear that out of the house, okay?"

"I won't," she said a tad too defensively.

Brandy wondered what she was "practicing" for. Middle school, she supposed. Why did that idea tie her stomach up in knots? Oh yeah, because middle school had been the worst years of her life and she wished to hell she could spare her kids all that weird social stuff that goes on in that age group.

Claire rooted through the grocery bags. "What's for dinner?"

"There's a roasted chicken in there. Unwrap it and put it on a plate for me, will you? And I'll make some broccoli to go with it."

She set a pan with a shallow amount of water on the burner to simmer while she finished unloading the groceries. She threw on a box of instant rice and 15 minutes later, they were sitting around the table, eating. She used to spend a lot of time cooking, but these days, it was pre-packaged or easy fare all the way.

"When are we decorating the tree, Mom?" Claire asked. Oh yeah. Right. Another thing on her to-do list. "As soon as I pull it out of the shed and set it up. This week, okay?"

"Can you buy eggnog?"

She smiled at her daughter, who loved all the holiday traditions. Trimming the tree together while dancing to Christmas songs and drinking eggnog had been their tradition from the time the kids were just toddlers. "Of course."

"So, mom," Sam said, shoveling rice in his mouth like a starved man, "how many kids will be at the football clinic?" His pale blonde hair was too long in front and fell over his right eye. She resisted the urge to stroke it back out of his face. He wasn't a little boy anymore.

"I'm not sure, why? Are you nervous?"

He shrugged. "Kinda. Will they all be my age?"

"Yes, it's only for eighth-graders."

"And they're picking for next year's teams based on how we do, right?"

"Yes. But they're also teaching skills. It's not just a try-out, so don't worry. Just go out there and play like it's any practice."

"Yeah, right," he muttered. After a few moments, he said, "Dad doesn't think I'm going to get in."

She set down her fork and stared at him, dinner suddenly sinking to the bottom of her stomach like a stone. "Excuse me?"

Sam lifted his shoulders again. "Yeah. He said he wanted me to be prepared. That I probably won't get in. He said I'd have a better chance if I were black. Is that true?"

31

She rolled her eyes. Leave it to Justin to plant these insidious seeds of doubt in their son's mind. "No, I don't believe that. I think you'll be judged based on how well you perform, not on the color of your skin. And you are a great player. You have a good throwing arm and you run fast. You may not be big yet, but that just means you're lighter and can get around the bigger guys."

Sam snorted. "I'm not sure that's how it works, mom."

Claire was listening with wide eyes. "Dad just doesn't want him to go to Houston High," Claire said.

From the mouths of babes.

At least she didn't have to say it. Her kids were smart enough to understand the dynamics without her having to bad-mouth their dad in front of them.

"Yeah, ever since I tested into the prep academy, that's all he talks about." Sam sounded bitter. "I wish I'd failed the test."

"Sam." She used her most admonishing tone. "Your father is just proud of you, that's all. But just because you tested into the school, doesn't mean you have to go there. If football is more important to you, we can make this happen."

"What about Dad?"

"Why don't you just concentrate on doing your best at the clinic? One step at a time, okay?" She forced a perky smile, even though her own stomach twisted with anxiety. It could be a major fight with Justin, who happened to be a lawyer and was quick to threaten to take her to court for whatever he wanted. Hopefully things wouldn't come to that. But she still was going to give him a piece of her mind after the kids went to sleep.

The kids helped her clean up from dinner and watched some television before bedtime. Part of her missed the nights of reading Harry Potter books to them before lights out, like when they were younger, but their new independence gave her more freedom, too. With Phenomenal Physiques, she needed all the time she could get.

She went into crazy organizational mode, folding laundry and taking care of all the odds and ends around the house. After the kids went to bed, she called Justin. When he picked up, she heard the din of voices in the background, as if he was at a bar.

"What's up?"

"Sounds like it's a bad time?"

"Kinda. What's up?"

"Sam says you told him he didn't have much of a chance of getting on the Houston High football team."

"Well, he doesn't," Justin snapped.

"How can you say that? Justin, you've seen him play. He's really good."

"Listen, I just don't want him to throw his education away on a physical sport. One injury and it could all be over—then where would he be? He's better off channeling that energy into intellectual pursuits."

"Justin, do you realize that Sam had to test to get into the Advanced Placement track at Houston High as well? Their AP program is just as elite as a prep school, only without all the snootiness that goes with it. So he wouldn't be throwing away his education. Not at all." She took a long, deep breath, wanting to phrase her thoughts in a way that wouldn't completely piss Justin off. "I understand you don't believe physical pursuits are important. I guess I wonder if you're taking your resentment of my career choices out on our son?"

"It's not always about you, princess." Justin used the sneering tone of his that always set her teeth on edge.

"I *realize* that. I'm just making sure."

"Get over yourself. Did you ever consider you're the one who should stop trying to live out her unfulfilled dreams through her son? Just because you didn't start working out until your midlife crisis doesn't mean you have to push your kids into every sport available."

Okay, yeah. This was going nowhere. As usual. And if she didn't end it immediately, she'd be seething.

"Well, just be sure you get him there on Sunday, and try not to destroy all his confidence on the way."

Justin hung up without responding, which was probably best. The conversation wasn't going to improve.

She ran her fingers through her hair and sighed. Justin was toxic. Sam needed a positive influence in his life.

Someone like Rick Morehouse. Because despite all his flirty player thing, everyone said he had a heart of gold.

She wanted him for Sam, just as a coach, of course. She wasn't thinking about dating him. Or about jumping his hot body. Nope, not at all.

* * *

Rick let himself into his condo and pulled off his jacket. His buddies thought it was funny he lived in a condo instead of a Houston mansion, considering he'd been paid $36 million by the Houston Texans before the nerve damage in his shoulder put him permanently out of professional ball. It had been the surgery for his severed rotator cuff that had actually ended his career. Somehow, nerves had been clipped and he couldn't even close his fist for a year afterward. His agent, mother and friends had wanted him to sue the doctor and hospital where the surgery had been done, but he'd taken it as a sign that it was time to move on. He'd never regretted that decision.

Anyway, he'd purchased that big mansion for his mother to live in, and she was happily retired now, living the life of leisure she never had when raising him. He preferred a condo, anyway. It was simple, like him.

Bachelor pad was what his mom called it, and she might be right. He wasn't ready for the house and the lawn and a wife and kids. He had plenty of young girls willing to go out with him on a less-than-serious basis. Or at least, when they pressured him to get serious, he found a new one.

He supposed he just hadn't met the right woman. Now that he'd met Brandy Love, he wondered if he hadn't been searching the wrong pool. Sure, the young women he dated were beautiful, but they lacked maturity, grace. They lacked the experience and spark that comes from living their life purpose. He recognized that spark in Brandy. She loved Phenomenal Physiques and she obviously worked very hard to make it successful. He loved that about her.

His physical attraction to her had been off the charts. He'd never wanted to turn Neanderthal and claim a woman as his own, fight any man who got between them and carry her off to ravish her. He closed his eyes remembering those bee-stung lips, the delicate curve of her throat, her muscular ass.

He shook his head as if it might clear the thoughts of Brandy and plopped down at his kitchen table where he dropped a manila folder stuffed with papers. A post-it note on the top said, *Call me. ~Phil.*

He picked up his cell phone and speed dialed Phil, the junior varsity football coach. They'd be working closely together on the three-week Sunday clinic for incoming freshmen. He'd started the clinic a few years ago because it gave them a chance to observe the boys over a longer period of time than just a single tryout, plus it gave the kids a leg up on skills so they started the new year ready to work hard and win.

"Hey man, what's up?" he said when Phil answered the phone. "I have the registration forms in front of me."

"So the deadline was yesterday and we received 108. We only have room for 80. What do you want to do?"

He blew out his breath. He didn't want to cut kids sight unseen. The whole point of the clinic was to have a chance to interact with the boys on a personal level before making any decisions for the next year. "What would it take to accommodate all of them? One more coach? I wonder if we can get a parent volunteer?"

"That's an idea," Phil said. "How about Jake Farrow? His son's a freshman—Lucas Farrow? On the

JV team? He's always around at practices—you'd recognize the guy if you saw him."

"Sounds good, will you contact him?"

"Sure thing. How'd it go with Donnie? Will he be ready for playoffs?"

"I'm not putting him in this week, but for sure by playoffs. I don't want to push him back in too soon and risk permanent damage of that knee. He'll need a doctor's sign-off, anyway."

"What does that mean for your game Friday night?" Phil sounded sympathetic. Donnie was the Tigers' star linebacker and running back and having him on the bench left a big hole on the team.

"Well... this will give the younger players a chance to step up."

Phil laughed. It was standard coach-speak to put an upbeat spin on a crappy situation. "Right. If anyone can bring them up, it will be you."

"Thanks, man. You going to poker night Friday at Dave's?" Dave was the assistant varsity coach, and he hosted a weekly poker night at his place.

"Planning on it, but I have to check with the boss." He meant his sweet and very pregnant wife, Amy. "She gets a little more possessive during football season. You know—it's a lot of time away from home." Phil also taught science at Houston High.

"Of course, no pressure. Tell Amy I said hi," he said.

"Will do. See you tomorrow."

"Thanks for organizing this."

"No problem. 'Night."

Rick hit the end button on his phone and opened the file folder, leafing through the stapled registration packets. They included the boys' permission slips, emergency contact information and proof of a doctor's physical. He wasn't looking for anything in particular—just names he recognized, like younger brothers of boys already on the team. He shuffled through the papers and stopped when a name caught his eye.

Brandy Love.

His Brandy Love? Well, not *his*, but yeah, he sure as hell had been thinking about her non-stop since they'd met a few days ago. He'd been dying to make her his. But this changed things. He scanned the paperwork. She had a kid? Yep. Sam Anderson.

For one horrible moment, he nearly choked. Was she married? Was that why she blew him off? But no... there hadn't been a ring. Did that mean she was divorced?

He checked the parent contact information. Yes, separate addresses for the two parents. But it really came as no relief. He didn't date single moms.

Ever.

It was one of his personal rules.

He'd grown up with an absentee father and a parade of his mom's boyfriends tromping through his life. Just when he'd get attached to one, it would be over. Seriously, the only stable male force he'd had in his life had been his high school football coach. It was probably why he'd poured every ounce of his energy into football, had worked so hard to become the very best and succeed. All for Coach Dinsmore. Or perhaps to prove something to his father, who'd never cared enough to take an active role in his life.

Yeah, when he'd become quarterback for the

Houston Texans, his father had flown out from Florida and suddenly tried to reclaim him as his son. He'd realized that in some way, his high school self had wanted that, had worked hard exactly for that scenario. Of course when it finally happened, he'd been utterly disgusted.

He read and re-read Sam Anderson's registration form, as if it might change things. But no, Brandy was Sam's mom, and that meant she was off-limits.

Too bad, because he already had a hundred fantasies running around his brain that involved her naked and showing off how flexible she was...

Chapter Four

"Who was that?" Jennie demanded as she watched Brandy's new colleague Adam Languard's jean-clad ass disappear through Phenomenal Physique's glass doors.

Brandy smiled. "Not bad looking, is he?"

"Please tell me he's a new hire."

"He is, sort of. A sub-contractor. He's going to bring Crossfit into Phenomenal Physiques."

"Yes!" Jennie gave a fist punch in the air.

"Oh, it gets even better. He says his twin brother is a firefighter and we should expect the entire squad up here working out."

Jennie rolled her eyes to the ceiling. "I've died and gone to heaven. When does he start?"

"Not until after the new year. We're going to convert Studio D into the Crossfit studio and I need to bring in some new equipment. Not much, though. That's the beauty of Crossfit."

"Happy new year to me. I can't wait." She reached for one of the brownies piled high on a plate. "Did you try these nutty ones?"

Jennie had organized a Christmas cookie exchange with all the employees, so they were all high on sugar after sampling so many.

"No, but I can't try any more. I'll bring them home for the kids."

Jennie looked toward the doors again. "Ooh, speaking of not bad looking...here comes another one."

It would be impossible not to notice Rick Morehouse walk into the gym. Even if he wasn't famous, the 6'5" quarterback with broad shoulders looked like he stepped out of a gladiator movie.

She wouldn't mind him tossing her over his shoulder to carry off as a war prize.

He strolled right up to the front desk with his student in tow and leaned his forearms on the counter. "Hullo, Ms. Love."

So. Damn. Charming. And probably so full of himself.

"Brandy," she corrected him. She planned to act professionally with him today, but her body had another idea. She had to wipe off the flirty smile that had involuntarily stretched across her face. She didn't even realize at first that she'd matched his pose, leaning on her forearms to meet him across the counter.

Without taking his green eyes off her, he slid a piece of paper across the counter in her direction. "Here's the liability waiver, signed by Donnie's mom. Are we clear to work out?"

Somehow his tone both implied she'd been silly to insist on the paperwork, and also that he'd been naughty not to bring it in the first place. Or she was imagining way too much about this interaction? Whatever the innuendos were, they had her pussy on notice, tingling, hoping that more than a little casual flirting would be going on.

Which it wouldn't.

She pulled on her all-business panties. "I set you up with a full membership, so you're in our system now and welcome to work out here any time." It had been a professional decision, really. Having Rick Morehouse working out in her club only raised the visibility and status of her place. He would definitely be good PR. It may have been a professional decision, but warmth crept up her cheeks as if she was still in high school and hoped the homecoming king would ask her on a date. Another one, since she'd dissed him the first time.

Ah, hell. She pulled back, not wanting Rick to get a bigger head. Of course, he was used to women blushing and throwing themselves at him.

His eyes dropped to her bustline as she moved and she realized she'd given him quite the cleavage shot. Well, the twins were looking particularly perky today, if she did say so herself. Not bad for a middle-aged mother who'd breastfed two children.

She made a point of ignoring his leer and peering around him. "Hi, Donnie."

The lanky youth smiled. "Hello Ms. Love."

Taking the hint, Rick stood back from the counter and sauntered into the studio with his student trailing behind him.

She exhaled, part relief at him walking away, part disappointment. Jesus, that man was full of himself. Someone should take him down a peg or two.

He dropped a hand on to Donnie's shoulder, leaning his head toward the kid, who was almost as tall as him. She couldn't hear the words, but it seemed apparent they shared a camaraderie or closeness. It made her smile. As she worked the front desk, she kept an eye on them, watching Rick run the boy through a series of exercises. She wasn't a football coach, but as a personal trainer, she approved of the workout he'd designed. She also liked the way both their faces broke into smiles frequently. As much as she wanted to reject Rick's charm, she had to admit he seemed like a nice enough guy.

In addition to a ladies' man. Which was why she would be taking his bait.

But she really hoped her son got onto his team. If he did, Sam would attend Houston High, for the sole purpose of playing football for Morehouse. If not, he'd go to Houston Prep Academy, the fancy private school her husband had picked out for him. It had taken a lot of arguing and cajoling just to get Justin to agree to this part, and it had only been because Sam had asked and not her that Justin had finally agreed.

Sam hadn't hit his growth spurt yet, but neither she nor his father were small, so she had no doubt by high school, he'd make a great player. In the meantime, he was a fast runner and quick at catching the ball. He'd played all three years of middle school and really loved the game. It was the one thing he was enthusiastic about, and she wanted to encourage it.

It wasn't that Sam was a bad student, but he didn't love schoolwork and it seemed like the more his father pushed him to improve his grades and prepare for college, the more he rebelled. It was like Justin wanted Sam to measure up to his school successes, and the more he talked about it, the more defensive Sam became. She hoped football would give him a reason to work hard. A coach like Morehouse could help him succeed, possibly even improve his grades.

Rick put the youth on the cycle and looked over at her.

Damn. Had he caught her watching? She started to turn away, but he'd already flashed her a grin and was walking over.

Oh stop—did her heart really have to pick up speed? She put on her most professional mask.

"Did I see your name on some paperwork for my football clinic this week?"

The mask dropped away and she brightened. "Yes. My son Sam will be participating."

Another toothpaste commercial worthy smile. "Well, I wanted to tell you he'll be in good hands."

"I'm sure he will." She willed herself not to beam back at him.

"Also, I just wanted to mention that I don't play politics, so if your son gets on the team, it will be on his merits alone."

Her eyes narrowed. What was he insinuating? That she was trying to buy her son's way onto the team?

As if he sensed he'd offended her, he winked and rushed on. "I tell all the parents that, to head them off before they start dropping off expensive gifts or home-baked muffins."

"Right. I'll cancel the massage I'd scheduled for you at 7:00, then." She made a show of looking at her watch. Immediately, she wished she'd picked something other than a massage, because the image of him lying naked on the massage table, and her oiled hands running all over his skin flashed in front of her eyes.

Please don't let him be imagining the same thing. Great, now he would assume she was offering sexual favors for her son's position on the team!

He just laughed, though, and looked back over at Donnie, whose head was bent as he rode the bike. "I'd better get back, I just wanted to tell you I'm looking forward to meeting your son."

It didn't seem like a come-on. But Rick Morehouse was very skilled at what he did. She just wasn't sure what all that charm meant.

* * *

Rick sent Donnie home and slipped into the empty studio where Brandy had been teaching the last time he was there. He pulled out the Bluetooth headset he'd picked up and set the receiver to scan for it.

"What are you doing?" The authoritative snap of Brandy's voice brought his head up. Her hands were on her hips and her brows drawn together.

He'd never really understood the "you're sexy when you're mad" notion until this moment. Brandy looked hotter than hell standing there with one hip cocked, her long blond ponytail hanging over one shoulder. Although you'd never guess it from the women he dated, he liked a strong woman, the kind who knew what she wanted and wasn't afraid to get it. And the kind who was willing to defend her turf.

He straightened and grinned. "Stealing your headset. I saw it was working *so* well last time…"

Her expression clouded and she walked over. She wore sneakers, but he had a flash fantasy of her dressed to the nines in high heels and a pencil skirt. She was the kind of statuesque woman who could make men fall to their knees before her.

Her brows shot up and she reached for the new

headset he held in his hand. "Where did this come from?" Confusion flitted across her face as she lifted her pale baby blues to meet his.

He shrugged. "Try it out. See if it works."

"Did you *buy me* a new headset?" She sounded incredulous.

"Yeah. I believe it's working now." He reached over and hit the on button, brushing her arm as he did. His skin tingled from the contact and the memory of her fingernails scraping along his lower back came flooding back, sending a surge of lust kicking through him.

"Are you serious? You bought me a new one? Why?"

He looked down at her in amusement. "Just wanted to return a favor. You're helping Donnie out... and all the underprivileged kids at the Fostering Christmas event. It's the least I can do."

Her mouth opened and closed and then, unaccountably, her beautiful eyes filled with tears.

His smile faded. "Hey..." The ice princess wasn't so tough afterall.

She blinked and looked away. When her gaze returned, her blue eyes had narrowed. "I'm still not going to date you."

Ouch. What the hell?

Her gaze faltered and pain flashed across her expression again. She shook her head, as if trying to clear it. "I mean—is that why you did this? Because my answer is still no."

His lip curled in annoyance. "Actually, I don't date the parents of kids I coach, so that is off the table."

She paled slightly. "Oh... of course. I'm sorry. I was rude. It's just that... no one—" she blinked rapidly. "I just don't understand your motivation." A few students filtered in and she glanced at them in distraction.

He shrugged. "My motivation was in being nice. You might try it some time."

Okay, that was harsh. She probably didn't deserve it. Based on the way she recoiled, he guessed his words had struck hard.

A few more of her students filtered in and she looked over and greeted them by name, turning her back on him.

Yep, that was his cue. He grabbed his bag and headed out, wondering why the hell he had even tried.

* * *

Brandy tapped on the door to her parents' house and pushed it open, letting herself in. "Hi Mom, hi Dad!" she called. She'd picked up takeout from Chipotle for them and she carried it into the kitchen.

"Shh," her mom said, meeting her there and taking one of the bags to unload. "Your father's still sleeping. He needs his afternoon naps."

Her father had had a stroke two years ago. It damaged his right side, so he used a walker now, because his foot dragged. He also hadn't fully regained his speech. Before the stroke, it was colon cancer, which he had kicked. The guy would live to be one hundred, if her mom had anything to do with it.

Taking care of her dad was her mom's full time project. It always had been. Her mom had devoted her entire married life to doting on her dad. Not that her

47

dad wasn't worth it. He was a great guy. He'd been a high school principal. Her mom had been the stay-at-home Susie Homemaker. The kind of wife Justin had wanted. The kind of wife he assumed he was getting. He'd probably figured he'd scored a homerun the day he met her parents—June and Ward Cleaver.

Brandy had fallen into the role easily because it had been familiar. She "got" the 1950's wife thing. But when the kids had gone to school and she sat at home wondering why she couldn't care about making the perfect soufflé, she knew something had to give. She wasn't her mother. She didn't want to be her.

She was just way more selfish, she supposed. She wanted her own life, separate from her husband's. She wanted to follow her own pursuits. And when Justin dug his heels in, the sensation of being trapped inside her mother's life overwhelmed her. She'd known she had to get out, at all costs. What her mom had loved, she'd come to despise.

Brandy always wondered what her mom might have done with her life, if she'd taken up a career. She was smart, incredibly capable, and good with people. She could've done or been anything. Even in a time when women's careers were limited to becoming a teacher or secretary. That doesn't mean Brandy didn't think her life had been well-spent. She'd had a wonderful childhood thanks to a stay-at-home parent. But her mother's shining example had only made her own stay-at-home years seem lacking in comparison.

At the moment, her mother was rattling non-stop about her father's food regimen. "... so I've been adding flax meal to his oatmeal in the morning, he seems to like that."

Yeah, right. She seriously doubted her dad liked flax meal in his oatmeal. But he would go along with anything her mother decided was best for him.

"Boo." The slurred sound of her father's weakened voice calling her pet name sounded from the hall. He moved slowly, pushing the walker.

Her eyes burned. He used to call out "Brandy-Boo, where are you?" when he got home from work when she was a kid. Now he had to work so hard just to sound out the single syllable.

She smiled and rushed down the hall to meet him. "Hi, Daddy." She kissed his cheek as his face crinkled into a smile. It was odd to have to bend over to meet his face, when he'd always been taller than she.

Her mother had also hurried forward, and she hovered nearby, ready to help him into his easy chair in the living room.

"Guess who has been coming to my gym?" she asked her father when he settled in his chair and her mom had brought him a glass of water with a straw.

"Wwho?" He took the time to round his lips, blowing extra breath across them to enunciate the word. Her mom had him working on a speech app on their iPad every day.

"Rick Morehouse."

His face lit up. He'd been a fan of Rick's when he played for the Texans, and now he followed Houston High's successes with enthusiasm. As a man who had made a career out of teaching in the public schools, he'd been delighted by Rick's choice to coach high school rather than college ball somewhere. "It shows his heart is in the right place. He could've picked money, but he chose the kids," he used to say.

"He made enough money," her mother would always interject.

The point was, Rick Morehouse had long been a topic of conversation in her parents' house.

Her dad flapped his good hand in the air, encouraging her to go on.

"He's helping one of his students rehab and he picked my place. Probably because I invited him to play Santa at the Fostering Christmas gift drive."

Her dad continued to smile broadly. He waved his hand some more, his brow furrowing. He made this face before speaking, as if he had to search his brain for the word, first. "Sam?"

She guessed at his question. "Yes, Sam's starting the Houston High football clinic this weekend. He's really excited."

Her dad's face relaxed and he smiled again and nodded his head, leaning back into the chair.

"You want the television on, George?" her mom asked, ever solicitous.

He looked at Brandy and raised his eyebrows.

"No, I'm not staying. I just stopped by to bring ya'll some dinner before I pick up the kids." She leaned down and gave him another peck on the cheek. "I'll see you two later, okay?"

Her dad smiled and nodded.

She gave her mother a kiss and hug, grateful her mom still had it in her to take care of her father's every need. She absolutely hated to wonder what would happen to her mom if her dad died first. She would have zero purpose in life.

It was sad. At least Brandy had purpose and direction, even if she didn't have love.

Chapter Five

Rick tapped on Dave's door and pushed it open without waiting for him to answer. He could already hear boisterous male voices inside. The Friday night poker night was gearing up..

"Hey, how's it going?" Dave called out when he entered. "Help yourself to the beer."

Dave, a bachelor like him, had the ultimate man-cave condo. Equipped with a dartboard, foosball table, pool table and giant 55-inch HD television, his place was always the meet-up locale. He hosted a weekly poker night, and they arranged all work-related—or pseudo work related—meetings to happen at his place.

Last year, after the boys took the State championship, he'd hosted a post-season victory party for the boys, buying them root beer and Mountain Dew and letting them go nuts with all his games.

"It's going." Rick grabbed a Dos Equis and squeezed a wedge of lime into the mouth of the bottle before shoving it through the neck to drop down into the beer. A tiny plastic Christmas tree stood on Dave's kitchen counter, probably his only holiday decoration. Not that Rick could throw stones. His mother had tried to get him to decorate, but he'd refused. That's what her place was for.

The usual suspects were all there—Dave and Phil, of course, Bill, a neighbor of Dave's, his brother-in-law, John, and Burt, the basketball coach from Houston High.

"What's the word?" he said by way of greeting to everyone.

"Hey, Rick," Phil called from the couch where he was playing Black Ops on the Xbox. "No!" he screamed at the screen, pitching his body to the left as he tapped the controller frantically. With his headset sitting slightly askew and his eyes bugging out at the screen, he looked half-maniacal.

Rick chuckled.

"Can you believe this shit?" Dave held up that day's copy of *The Houston Chronicle*. He hadn't looked but he'd already heard that Stan Brown, the King of Douchebaggery, aka the sports columnist, had lambasted him again over the way he'd coached last night's game. The guy's kid went to Coral Heights, Houston High's biggest rival, and he had it out for Rick and Houston High. The way things looked now, they'd probably be playing Coral Heights for the playoffs, which meant it would only get uglier from here. Texans took football seriously, even at the high school level. An entire stadium had been rented out for the playoffs in a few weeks, and the press was hot on everything to do with them.

"I've told you before not to read that rag. Nothing good will come of it."

"I think we should throw bags of dog shit on the douchebag's porch steps," Phil yelled from the living room. His voice was way too loud, even for calling from another room, probably from the adrenaline of playing the game.

"Or cut his cable line." Burt chuckled. He'd been on the receiving end of Stan's vindictive columns too.

Rick rolled his eyes. "He's just mad we beat Raven Ridge, even without our best linebacker. He was hoping his son's team would be up against Raven Ridge instead of us for the playoffs."

"Well, that's obvious." Dave slapped the paper down, sending the stack of paper napkins fluttering to the floor. "Oops." He bent to pick them up.

Curiosity got the better of Rick. "So what did I do wrong this time?"

"Well, it turns out you're only in the game for your own ego and you don't care about kids getting hurt. He predicts you'll be putting your star linebacker Donald Fleming back in the game too soon," Dave said.

"Jesus, can't we sue him for libel or something? I mean, he just makes shit up!" Phil yelled, then followed it by a series of expletives and finally, "Got you, motherfucker!"

"Right? It's not even like anyone got hurt last night. How did he even segue into that comment?"

"Read it," Dave prompted, shoving the paper toward him.

He started to pick it up, but good sense prevailed. "Not going to do it. I decided a long time ago never to let this stuff get to me. If I read it, I'm only going to get pissed off and then after we get a few beers in us, we'll all be down at the dickwad's house pissing on his lawn."

"Can we do that anyway?" Dave asked.

The guys laughed and Burt lifted his beer to clink his. "Hear, hear."

"Come on, let's play some cards," Rick said.

"Wait, wait, wait, wait... *yes!*" Phil shouted from the couch. He was pounding his feet on the floor, probably annoying the hell out of whoever lived below.

"Phil, you can join us for the next round," Rick advised. "We wouldn't want to keep you from killing anyone."

"Take that you... oh *fuck*." Phil tore off his headset. "It's okay, I died. Let's play."

The guys gathered around the table and Rick picked up the cards to shuffle. "I'll deal."

Phil sat down beside him, carrying two fresh Dos Equis, wedges of lime stuffed in the mouths. He pushed one toward Rick. "Here you go."

"Thank you, sir." He slid the cards across the table, dealing. "Everything set for the clinic Sunday?"

"Yep, I got Jake Farrow, a parent volunteer lined up, we're good to go. Did you look at the forms? Anyone interesting?"

"One kid. I don't know him, but his mom is Brandy Love, the owner of Phenomenal Physiques. She's been letting me work out with Donnie there for free."

"Hope he's good," Dave said with a wry smile. "Be a shame to burn that bridge."

He hoped the kid was good, too. Not because he wanted to keep using Brandy for her gym. Because for some reason, he already cared about her kid.

But that was stupid. Brandy was not his woman, nor would she ever be, no matter how many times he fantasized about having her. Which meant he should not be especially invested in her kid.

Too bad his heart never seemed to cotton onto his logical mind's decisions.

* * *

Brandy sighed and flipped off the lights left on by the last teacher who used the back studio. Everyone had gone for the night and she was closing up. She only closed on Saturdays, when the kids spent the night at their dad's.

And yes, that was why she didn't have time for a love life. Because when in the hell would she ever go on a date?

The sound of water dripping in the men's locker room made her sigh. Someone had left a faucet on again. It drove her crazy. The cleaning people would probably turn it off when they came, but she didn't want to leave it running—she paid the water bill here, and some months it cost her a fortune.

She pushed open the door. All the lights were still on, too. Good thing she checked.

As she zipped around the corner toward the showers, the water abruptly stopped and her mouth dropped open in shock.

Holy hardbody, Batman!

A naked, muscled, hot man stood dripping wet in front of her, his face—and only his face—covered with his towel as he wiped water from his head.

Coach Perfect.

Lord help her, he was even more stunning with his clothes off.

The towel lowered and piercing green eyes fixed on her.

The proper thing to do would be to turn and hightail it out. Or to at least avert her eyes. To apologize profusely. But she seemed to have frozen. She couldn't even bring her hand up to cover her gaping mouth.

Rick's lips curved into sexy smirk. He didn't move to cover himself as he padded toward her. The soft splash of his flip-flops on the wet tile seemed to echo, almost as loudly as the beating of her heart.

Her eyes traveled down the length of his body, resting on his hardening cock, which was huge, like the rest of him.

"What's wrong?" he drawled in his deep, sexy voice, "The water in the women's locker room too cold?"

She took one step back from him as he continued to advance. She didn't trust herself if she got in touching distance of that... naked... *hard*....

She jerked her eyes back up to his face. "I... uh... I'm sorry. I was just locking up. I didn't realize you were in here."

He cocked his head. "I don't know, you look a little dirty to me." He was in her personal space now, right in front of her, naked and gleaming. "Come on in here, let me wash you off."

She literally swayed on her feet as the blood rushed out of her head and flooded the area about two feet south. And then her hands were on his wet chest, rubbing water droplets through the soft curling hairs.

He covered her hands, captured them, not letting her pull away. He took one in his own and pulled her toward the shower, as if serious about washing her off.

"Rick... I, uh..." She dragged her feet a little, offering a show of resistance.

"Shh." He snaked an arm around her waist and pulled her against him, dampening her clothes with the moisture on his body. His lips came down and crushed hers, shutting her up, overpowering her, until her head swam and all rational thought fled her mind.

She looped her arms around his neck and kissed him back with more ardor than she knew she had in her.

God, his lips were soft and strong. He sucked at hers, licked into her mouth. One hand came up to cup the back of her head and he held her in place for his onslaught.

Against her belly, his cock thickened and twitched.

She sighed and moaned and he captured them all with his lips, devouring her as his tongue thrust into her mouth.

Suddenly the water was on, spraying them both, soaking her hair and clothes. She steadied herself by wrapping her arms around his neck, never stopping with the frantic kissing as she toed off her sneakers.

He yanked her yoga top off over her head and his expression as he reached for her breast took her breath away.

Hunger.

Shock. Pleasure. Worship. Satisfaction.

She read it all on his face as he crushed her breast and lifted it to his mouth. He was too rough, and she loved every minute of it. She'd never felt "overpowered" by a man before—had never wanted to—but this... this was amazing.

He nipped and sucked at her nipple, laved it with his tongue until both breasts swelled and ached, nipples standing out in stiff peaks. Then he was at the other breast, teasing and torturing it.

Her hips snapped forward and she arched under his hands.

He slid his thumbs in the waistband of her stretch pants and dragged them down, squatting to help her step out of them.

"Oh hell, yeah," he muttered as he lifted his torso, his eyes on her neatly trimmed mons. His fingers arrived there before he'd fully stood, exploring her slippery heat.

She gasped, bucking at his confident touch.

Yes, Rick Morehouse knew his way around a pussy. That should have made her brain throw the brakes back on, but it didn't. Because it. Felt. Wonderful. His fingers were large and he rubbed from her dewy entrance up to her pulsing clit and back again.

Heat poured off her in waves, and the steam around them couldn't just be from the shower.

His mouth attacked hers again, his hand gently tugging her head back with her hair.

With another guy, she might have been offended by the rough touch—but he awoke pure animalistic passion in her.

"Mmm," she crooned as his lips twisted over hers. One finger delved inside her. She hooked an arm around his neck because her knees were in serious danger of buckling.

He shoved her back against the cool tile and penetrated her with two fingers now. His hands were so large the digits filled her completely.

She bit her lips and moaned, rocked her hips to meet his thrusts.

He dropped to a crouch again and lifted one of her legs, throwing it over his shoulder. Even though she guessed what he was going to do, she was unprepared for the shock as his tongue hit her clit.

She gasped and gripped his wet hair, pulling hard.

"That's it, angel," he murmured. "Take your pleasure."

She tipped her pelvis toward his face and cried out hoarsely.

He shoved his fingers deep inside her, hitting the magic g-spot.

"Oh, God," she whined. "Oh, please."

"Take it."

He sucked her clit, licked it, flicked it all the while pumping his thick digits.

She came unglued. No, she just *came*. Hard. With a keening wail that filled the locker room and echoed off the walls, she took every bit of pleasure Coach Perfect offered. Her muscles clamped down, squeezing his fingers in pulsing waves.

Her foot slipped, but Rick had her, pinning her pelvis up against the wall, not letting her fall, or rest until every last bit of pleasure had been wrung out of her. When the orgasm had finally passed, she sagged, her limbs like rubber, unable to move or think or speak.

Rick stood slowly, a satisfied smirk on his face. He reached beside her head and turned off the water. "You're beautiful when you come," he murmured, his eyes heavy-lidded, as if drunk on her pleasure.

She blushed like a schoolgirl. Had he been watching her while she came? That was embarrassing. Well, two could play at that game. She reached for his cock but he caught her wrist and pressed it back against the tile wall by her head.

"Uh uh." He leaned in and kissed her again, a sensuous exploring of her lips. When they broke apart, he gave a lazy smile. "That was for you. Because you don't get enough help around here."

She pushed her wet hair from her eyes. "I'm happy to return the favor." She licked her lips, making sure he saw her tongue take a slow ride around her mouth.

His eyes darkened and his cock stiffened even more, but to her surprise, he shook his head. "No... I'd like it better if you owed me one."

Her brows drew together, her post-orgasmic mind not following him. "What?"

He kissed her again, which didn't help the fuzzy brain situation. "You said you're not dating right now. And I'm really not, either. But everybody can use a little *help*... in or out of the shower now and then." He reached for his towel, which at some point had magically ended up back on the hook. Grabbing the corners, he wrapped it around her.

Warmth and languor flowed through her body, the bliss of her orgasm leaving her open and receptive to anything he had to say, even though she still didn't quite follow.

"I guess I don't want this to be our one and only hookup," he explained, his husky voice spiking a renewed shiver of need through her "That was hot—*smoking* hot. And I want a repeat. Soon. So I'm gonna walk out of here with you owing me."

That shit-eating smirk was all over his face again. He knew he was the cat's meow with women. He could pretty much tell her anything right then and she'd accept it.

Who was she to argue with his logic? It wasn't dating, it was a hookup. He wanted a booty call.

Nothing wrong with that. If neither of them was looking for a relationship, then no one would get hurt. She wrapped the towel around her waist, a choice he obviously appreciated, based on the flick of eyebrows at her bare breasts.

"You want me to owe you, huh?" She adopted a flirty tone.

"Yes, ma'am."

"All right, Coach. You're up by one point. Be ready for me, I'll be practicing my moves."

He threw back his head and laughed, the deep baritone filling her chest with pleasure.

She bent to pick up her soaked clothes, but he beat her to them. "I've got it. My treat, remember? You're not working here tonight."

She laughed, ripples of pleasure flowing through her. "You are something else, big guy."

He wrung her clothing out and gave her a sheepish grin. "I have a spare T-shirt in my gym bag.

"That's okay, I keep extra clothes here."

He wrapped his thick arm around her waist again and pulled her in for another kiss. "Thank you," he murmured when they broke apart, although she couldn't figure out why he'd be thanking her when she was the sole beneficiary of their activities. "That was nice."

"I believe I'm the one who does the thanking here." She stood on her tiptoes to initiate another kiss.

He squeezed her ass through the towel as she did,

sending a fresh shot of desire coursing through her. But there would be a next time. Possibly many next times. Without the constraints of a relationship.

Yes, this arrangement had success written all over it.

All she had to do was hang onto her heart.

* * *

Brandy broke away from him and smiled. She looked absolutely beautiful. Of course, she always was a knockout, but right now she wore that "just fucked" flush with the bright, dilated eyes and a relaxed and peaceful expression. He wanted to see that face on her on a daily basis.

That was probably asking too much, but he'd take whatever he could get. Brandy Love rocked his world.

She glided toward the door, wearing nothing but his towel around her waist.

"Hang on a second." He dug in his gym bag and pulled out a clean T-shirt. "I don't want you walking out there like that. What if there's some other guy still hanging around somewhere?"

She laughed, a husky musical sound, and caught the shirt when he tossed it. She slid it on and it fell over her like a dress, far too large. Somehow, she looked even sexier to him in his T-shirt, her long, muscular legs framed by the hemline. Possibly he just liked seeing her in something he owned, as if it somehow marked her as belonging to him.

Too bad that wouldn't ever happen because the more he was around her, the more fascinating she became.

She stepped out and he pulled on his own clothes, thanking his lucky stars he'd decided to come for a late night workout instead of going to a bar with Dave. He swiftly tied his shoelaces and headed out, wanting to help her with whatever else she needed to do to lock up.

He found her flicking off a few more lights.

"No other guys waiting around to surprise you?" He said it lightly, but it occurred to him that he didn't like her locking up alone here at night.

"Nope." She dug for her keys in her purse.

"I'll walk you out. Do you close up every night?"

"No, just Saturdays when my ex has the kids."

He made a mental note to be there every Saturday night—and not just for sex. She needed to have a guy around to make sure she got to her car safely.

They walked down the stairs and out to the parking lot. Her car was in a reserved space right up front. That came as a small comfort to him. At least it was well lit and close to the building.

He pushed her up against the door of her car and stole one more kiss before he said good night. "Will I see you tomorrow?"

He didn't blame her for looking confused. She'd just had steamy hot shower sex with a guy she didn't know well enough—yet. "For the football clinic?"

"Oh!" she flushed. "Justin—my ex—will drop Sam off, but I'll be there to pick him up."

"Okay. We'll take good care of him."

She reached out and touched his chest with one finger, sending a zing of excitement straight to his already blue balls. "I will hold you to that, Coach."

One more kiss. She tasted so good.

"Goodnight, Ms. Love." He opened her door for her and waited while she got in.

"Goodnight, Coach."

He shut the door and walked to his car, the taste of her still on his tongue.

Wow. He couldn't wait to have her again, even though he knew he definitely shouldn't.

Shower sex had presented a loophole in his personal rule about single mothers. It wasn't the same as dating. And Brandy had said she wasn't dating right now, so it was clearly just a hookup for her, too. She was mature enough to understand the difference between the booty call and a relationship.

He needed to be careful, though. Brandy was the last person he wanted to hurt.

Or get hurt by.

Chapter Six

The next day, Brandy yanked the boxes of Christmas decorations out of the shed with her cell phone trapped between her ear and her shoulder. Dang, this position had been easier before cell phones came along. Now she'd need a massage after hanging up. Of course, she had a Bluetooth somewhere. Somewhere being the operative word.

"So how's the job search?" she asked Meg.

Meg just groaned. "It's not just a job search, it's a career search. That's what makes it so hard. I don't need to work at Starbucks, I want a serious, career job, only I've been out of the work force for 15 years, so it seems nearly impossible. What made me decide to do this again?"

"You decided—in therapy—remember why?"

Meg made a groaning sound in her throat.

"So you're not depending on Teddy to fulfill all your needs."

"No, I decided so I'd have a means to support myself if we get divorced. And he's not ringing any bells in any of the needs departments these days," she grumbled.

"Are we talking about sex here?"

"Yes."

"Have you thought about seducing him?"

"I don't even want to. I'm so mad at him. I think—I think we're going to try a separation."

Brandy sucked in her breath. "Wow. You already talked about that?"

"Yeah. He would move out. He's looking at some condos by the hospital."

"Are you okay?"

"Yes, I'm fine. It was my suggestion."

"Have you told the kids?"

"No, not yet. We only just started talking about it. Brandy... he seemed relieved." Her voice broke.

"That doesn't mean he wants this. Honestly... you haven't asked my opinion, but I'm not sure either of you want this. I think you both just realize something has to change."

Meg sniffed. "I don't know," she wailed. "I really don't."

"Well, just don't rush into anything. If you try the separation, maybe just tell the kids that Daddy needs to stay closer to work for a while because he's really busy."

"That won't be hard for them to believe," she said dryly. His long surgeon's hours were a major source of their discord.

"How would you like to take on the event coordination for Phenomenal Physiques? Not as my employee, but as an independent contractor? So it'd be your own business? I'm in over my head with trying to launch the new stores. I could really use someone like you to help me plan the parties. The Fostering Christmas thing is just around the corner and I don't even have a clue what I'm doing, yet."

"Really?"

"Yeah." She dropped the last box of decorations in her living room and sighed. She wished Meg was over here right now to decorate for her. She was good at these sorts of things. They only stressed Brandy out.

"That sounds fun."

"Well, think about it. I could really use your help."

"Thanks, I will." She sounded a few shades brighter. "Is that why you called?"

"No."

"Well, what's up?"

She opened the box holding the fake Christmas tree and dumped the plastic pine-needled branches out on the carpet. "I had hot monkey sex with Rick Morehouse last night."

"*Get. Out.*"

"Serious."

"Seriously serious? So what happened? Where? What's the scoop?"

"It's crazy. I was locking up and I found him naked in the men's showers." She sorted the branches into stacks according to the color on their ends.

"Oh yeah, *suuure,* you did."

She laughed. "It's true. I thought everyone was gone, but I heard water running, so I went in to see if someone had left a faucet on. There he was. In living color."

"Oh mah *gawd*, Brandy. This is the best story I've heard since... well, I don't know when." Meg's southern accent always became stronger when she gossiped, as if she was channeling her mother.

"We're not dating, though. We both agreed. Just

sex." Branches organized, she started assembling the tree.

Meg sniffed. "And why is that?"

"I already told you. I don't have time for a relationship. But that doesn't mean I don't have certain *needs*." She giggled.

"How was he? Was he any good?"

"He was amazing. Like, the best I've ever had."

"So was it just a one-time thang?"

"Mmm, no, he angled for more. He's totally a player, but I figured this works for me. Hot sex, no commitment. What could be wrong with that scenario?"

Meg made an indistinct sound, as if she might disagree but didn't want to say so. "Brandy, how about we make a deal?"

"What deal?"

"If I keep an open mind about saving my marriage, you keep an open mind about dating Rick Morehouse. He'd be perfect for you. Brandy, I *want* him for you."

Something stirred in her chest—one part discomfort, one part pleasure. Did she want him for herself, too? She gave herself a shake. "No deal. I'm seriously not ready to date."

"It's been four years since your divorce."

"Not ready."

Meg sighed. "Well, I still want him for you. That's not going to change."

She inserted the last branch in the "trunk" and surveyed her work. "Well, thanks, I guess."

"You're welcome. And thanks for the job suggestion. I'm going to mull it over."

"You do that. We'll talk soon."

"Yes. I'll call you tomorrow. Have a great day!"

She bid Meg the same and turned her phone off, rubbing the crick in her neck.

I want him for you.

Nope. It couldn't happen. Not now.

* * *

Sam Anderson was easy to spot at the clinic with his shock of blond hair, exactly the same color as his mother's. It hung over one eye in the modern version of the skater's cut. He was small, but most boys his age still were. His father dropped him off, and Rick strolled over to introduce himself.

"Rick Morehouse, head coach." He stuck out his hand.

The guy was tall, but lanky, with a slight belly. His skin was pasty, as if he spent all his time indoors. He looked down his nose at Rick and hesitated a moment before sticking out his hand. "Justin Anderson. This is Sam. We're really not sure if he's interested in playing next year—"

Sam frowned.

His father ignored it, "—but we agreed he could come and try it out for the clinic."

Rick decided to ignore the asocial father and smiled, instead, at Sam. "Have you played ball before?"

Sam nodded. "I've played all three years at Harlon Middle School."

"Oh yeah? What position?"

The boy looked up and met his eye squarely. "QB."

His eyebrows shot up. "That's great, son. You're going to be working with Coach Jones over there." He pointed to Dave. "Did you bring a water bottle?"

"Oh," the boy started. "I left it in the car."

His father rolled his eyes, looking put out. He handed him the keys. "Go and get it."

When Sam had left, Justin folded his arms across his chest and looked out at the field.

Rick should just walk away—this guy didn't deserve his attention, after all. But curiosity kept him standing there. *This* was the type of guy Brandy had picked in the past? He seemed like an asshole with a capital A.

"Sam's too little to play. His mom wanted him to do this. Personally, I wouldn't be brokenhearted if he didn't make the team. Like I said, we're not even sure he'd accept a spot if offered. He's tested into Houston Prep Academy." He said it proudly. Rick half-expected him to start reciting his kid's test scores to make up for his penis size, which had to be miniscule considering all the arrogance he was throwing out. But no, it was sweet he was proud of his kid, and if he was honest, he'd admit the only reason it rubbed him wrong was because this was Brandy's ex.

"Well, this clinic is good skill-building whether he makes the team or not." He stuck to the party line, resisting the temptation to mention that he'd already discussed Sam's chances of getting on the team with his ex-wife.

Intimately.

No, he didn't need to show his dick-size to this guy. He was comfortable with who he was and what he did.

Sam ran back up with the water bottle, breathless.

"All right, Sam, head on over to Coach Jones, over there." He pointed.

A far friendlier father came over to talk to him and he was saved from any more conversation with Justin Anderson. When he finished, he headed off to the grass, where the boys all sat waiting for instructions.

He had 108 boys to watch, but he kept an eye on Sam. The kid appeared to be working hard and giving it his best. Most boys at this age were awkward, and Sam was no exception, but when one of the coaches spoke to him, he listened intently and nodded immediately, so it appeared he had a good attitude.

Dave and Jake, the parent volunteer coach ran them through a series of warm-ups and drills, while he and Phil pulled kids out one by one for skill testing. The next two hours were a hectic blur. They didn't even get through one-third of the kids for individual testing by the time the practice was over.

"Okay, boys, huddle up in your groups."

He'd divided the boys into three groups, each with their own coach, so he'd be free to walk around and see all of them. He walked over to Sam's group now. Dave was their coach, and he was giving them the end of the day pep talk.

"How'd it go for you all today?" Rick asked.

The boys looked worn out, some of them rested doubled over with their hands on their knees, heads hanging. They had run them around with conditioning exercises for two hours straight.

Sam straightened and put his hands on his hips, still appearing out of breath. He nodded with the other boys.

"All right, you're dismissed. Give it to me, here." He put his palm up for them to slap a high five as they filed away. Sam was at the end of the line. "Good job, Sam."

The kid looked up, as if surprised to be called out by name, and then flushed with pleasure. "Uh..thanks, Coach."

He sensed her presence before he heard the sound of her voice. "Hey champ, how'd it go?"

His skin prickled with the memory of her naked in the shower the night before. But her kid was here, and he wasn't going to confuse him by acting overly-friendly toward her. God, he'd hated it when guys came onto his mom while he was standing right there. He remembered being Sam's age and wanting to throat-punch them.

Brandy had stopped with Sam a few feet away, asking him about his day. She had a young girl with her, around age ten or 11 but already as beautiful as her mother. Brandy looked up and flashed him her heart-stopping smile.

His body responded instantly, cock hardening in his pants.

Damn, this woman was dangerous. And her kid was *right there*.

He grit his teeth and gave her a bland, impersonal smile, lifting his hand to wave.

Surprise flittered across her features. "How'd it go, Coach?" she called out.

Ah, hell. He really didn't want to go over there and talk to her. He wouldn't be able to play it cool.

He gave her an inattentive wave again. "Real good," he called out over his shoulder, walking away from her. Yes, it was a Class A blow off, but he didn't want it to seem like he knew her any better than any other parent picking up their kid. Like he'd cupped her tits in his hands. Or had seen the way her face screwed up right before she came.

He distracted himself by talking shop with Phil and Dave until the field had cleared. But when he got in his Escalade to drive home, a nagging voice said he'd been an ass. But surely she'd understand? They'd already talked about not dating. They were a casual hookup, nothing more.

Too bad that pestering voice kept eating away at him.

He'd fucked up.

He hoped there wasn't hell to pay. Hadn't this been precisely what he wanted to avoid? Someone getting hurt?

* * *

Brandy drew in her breath and lifted her chest when Coach Morehouse stepped through the glass doors to the gym. It was only 9:30 in the morning—she certainly hadn't expected to see him at this time of day. She'd spent the last 24 hours hardening every part of herself toward him, and she was not about to get the pants charmed off her again.

The way he'd dissed her at the practice had been unforgivable. She'd been nauseous afterward. She'd never wanted to undo a one-night-stand more than theirs. It seemed she'd been right about Rick all along—he was a shallow, self-important player and she'd been dumb enough to get played.

It's not that she'd expected him to ask her on a date or call her up afterward, but she hadn't expected to be treated like she was invisible. Or like it just hadn't happened.

Despite their mutual vow to that they were only interested in a casual sex hook-up, she'd still expected to be treated... well, if not *special*, then with a little more warmth and charm than he'd shown out there. She wasn't a diva, but... sheesh. She deserved a little more polite attention than that!

She purposely bent over to file something as he sauntered up to the front desk, hoping he'd just pass on by. She'd caught the smile he flashed her. Ugh. It looked so damn genuine. Now she understood. He just played to get what he wanted. He played sweet to get free access to her club, played charming to nail her against a shower wall.

No, none of that rang true, and she really didn't want to regret their hook up. She'd used him as much as he used her. Heck, he hadn't even gotten off.

"How did your son like the clinic?" Rick asked brightly.

She straightened and arranged her features into what she hoped looked cool but pleasant.

Professional.

"He had a great time, thank you." She tried to make the *thank you* sound dismissive, so he'd walk away, but he didn't take the hint.

"Well, I haven't tested him, but he looked like he worked hard and brought a good attitude."

For her son's sake, she mustered a cheerful smile. "Glad to hear it." In an effort to get rid of him, she walked around the counter. She'd read that somewhere once—how to get rid of colleagues who stand in your office shooting the shit. You're supposed to stand up like you're leaving. "I'd better get to the studio for my next class," she said, when he didn't move.

Rick may be charming, but he wasn't stupid. She caught his recognition of her coolness in the way he studied her, some of his cheeriness fading away. "I'll catch up with you after your class?" He looked serious, like he was scheduling a real appointment.

She made an indistinct noise, giving him a blank but pleasant expression as she passed him and headed toward Studio B. She should've just said she wasn't available. But she didn't want him to catch her in a lie, since she didn't have anything scheduled. She needed to think of some pressing appointment fast.

She didn't exhale until she reached the empty studio and closed the door. The sight of the headset Rick had bought her sent a shard of pain rattling through her chest.

No, she was a big girl. She could handle awkward. She certainly had been a willing participant in the extracurricular shower activities, she would have to manage the fallout.

She taught her class on autopilot, the words coming out but without her awareness of even what she'd said. Her morning class was full of her regulars—the same diehards who never missed. They didn't need any special help or encouragement, so it worked out fine.

After class, she found Coach Charming shooting the shit with Jennie at the front desk. His hair looked wet around the edges, as if he'd just freshly showered and he'd changed into street clothes. In fact, he looked even more dapper than ever in his button down shirt and slacks.

Though she had no right to be jealous, it immediately set her teeth on edge to see their heads bent together.

"Oh! You know which one is really great?" Jennie leaned forward across the desk. "That South American restaurant, Americas, with the Gaudi-esque decor? Have you been there?"

It was one of Brandy's favorite lunch spots and it irritated the hell out of her to hear them making a lunch date there.

Not. My. Business.

Hopefully if she told herself that enough times it would sink in.

Rick's head lifted and he smiled at her. "There she is!"

Please, just shut up.

"I was just asking Jennie where you might like to go for lunch."

I'm sure you we— Wait... really? It was a pleasing idea for a nanosecond, but then she remembered why that would be impossible. Everyone in the gym would be talking about her and Mr. Eligible Bachelor. She'd be the talk of the town in no time. Besides, she hadn't forgiven him for being a dickwad at practice.

"That's sweet, but I really can't."

Rick's expression grew serious. "There are a few things I really need to discuss with you. About the Christmas event." Once again, she noted that he was no dummy. He clearly understood her desire to avoid gossip. "I just figured it would be easier at lunch, but if you prefer your office?" He gestured toward her office behind the front desk.

No, it would be better to be in a restaurant with him than sitting in that glass-walled office where all her customers and employees could see.

"You're right, lunch would be better. I'll go change my clothes and grab my purse."

She headed to the women's locker room where she kept a spare set of clothes and changed swiftly into a skirt, blouse and sandals. She applied a dash of lipstick, then cursed herself for trying. This was not a date. Not even close.

She met Rick at the front door and he smiled. He extended a hand like he was going to escort her with it at her back, but she stepped quickly ahead, swinging the glass door open too hard.

She made the mistake of looking back at Rick, who appeared amused.

Damn him, anyway.

"Shall we take separate cars so you don't have to return here afterward?" she suggested.

His brow furrowed. "No, I don't mind driving—"

"I'll drive," she cut in crisply.

Once more, he appeared amused. "I like a woman who drives," he murmured.

She scowled at him, flouncing to her eight-year-old Lexus SUV and hitting the door locks on her key fob.

He climbed in the passenger side and adjusted the seat back as far as it went to accommodate his long legs. He seemed to fill the vehicle, and not just because he was large. His presence was so magnetic, so intoxicating. Just the fresh smell of soap on his skin reminded her of their shower and the harder she tried to push it out of her mind the more it loomed there, right in the forefront.

That had been a mistake. A big one.

She started the vehicle, then inwardly cursed as the car groaned when she eased out of the parking space. It had just started doing that, and she hadn't had a chance to take it to the shop yet.

"Sounds like your power steering is going."

"I know, I know. I need to take it to the shop." She hated that she couldn't keep up with her life. She also hated for anyone else to see that part of her. Yeah, she might have a trace of her mom's perfectionism. The woman could write a five-page essay on the way the vacuum cleaner cord should be wrapped around the machine.

He shifted, angling his legs toward her as she pulled out into traffic.

The air between them became charged. Her skin tingled with his closeness.

After a moment of silence, he said, "I screwed up. Royally."

Her breath hitched in her chest. She kept her eyes glued to the road, navigating traffic. Although it had sounded like a come on, the fact that Rick didn't mind her driving said something about him. Justin had always insisted that the man was supposed to drive. If she did happen to be driving, her ex constantly made comments about female drivers and all the things they do wrong.

She didn't answer Rick, just waited for him to go on.

"I..." He shoved his fingers through his hair. "I

didn't want Sam to guess—you know—there was anything between us. And I wasn't sure I could hide it. I mean, what happened Saturday night was... *so hot.*" He sounded almost in awe.

Her heartbeat picked up speed, thudding against her ribs.

"But I sort of gave you the brush-off, and I'm sorry. I didn't mean to act like an asshole."

She wished she didn't care so much, but his words sent syrupy warmth through her chest. It made sense. He had been trying to play it cool and he'd overplayed it.

"Yeah, I don't want Sam to suspect anything, either, but I didn't expect you'd act like we'd never met."

"I know. I'm really sorry. It was a rookie move."

"But you're not a rookie." There was a challenge there, she supposed. Rick Morehouse was known for being a player and she wanted to hear what he had to say about it.

* * *

He loved the way Brandy kept his balls in a vise. He'd seen her icy exterior soften—suspected he was two-thirds of the way to forgiveness already, but he found her strong, assertive woman persona a total turn-on.

Like the way she insisted on driving.

"You're right, I'm not a rookie. I'm just..." He hesitated. He didn't often tell people about the not-so-pretty parts of his life. But Brandy deserved an explanation. "I'm touchy when it comes to kids. I actually don't date single moms, as a rule."

Her eyebrows shot up and he feared he'd offended her so he rushed on, into his story. "I was raised by a single mom, and she dated a lot of men. I mean a *lot* of men. They would come into my life and then she'd kick them out, or they'd walk out. I got hurt a lot. Some of them I liked, and it broke my heart when they left. Some of them I hated and wanted to kick out the door myself. The point is, I don't want to be that guy."

She pulled into the parking lot of the restaurant and looked over at him, her big blue eyes soft. "I'm sorry—that must've sucked."

He shrugged. "You know who was always there for me?"

"Who?" Her pouty lips rounded into a circle on the *oo* in who. He wanted to kiss her.

"My coach. Dale Dinsmore. That's why I coach high school instead of college ball. Because that's the guy I'm gonna be."

"That's the guy you are." Her voice was gentle. She'd forgiven him.

Now he just had to make sure she was going to give him another chance. Because he'd been looking forward to their next encounter since the second their last one ended.

He flashed a smile at her. "Shall we go eat?"

"Sure." She opened her door and swiveled her long, shapely legs out of the vehicle.

He walked around to meet her, but, of course, she didn't wait for him to shut her door. Their hands brushed and he reached to hold hers, but she shook him off. "This is business, remember? The last thing I need is for the press to start gossiping about us dating."

"I understand. Especially since we're not dating." At least they were on the same page with that part. It would be harder if she wanted to date and he had to let her down because of her kids.

He managed to beat her to the door of the restaurant and held it open for her, loving the way her lips curved up into a sexy acknowledgement of the game they played. The restaurant was incredible, with tiled sloping walls, just like a Gaudi building in Barcelona. They sat near a window and she put her napkin on her lap.

"Is that why you don't date?" he asked when they'd given their drink orders and the waitress had left a plate of plantain chips with an olive oil and lemon dip in the middle of the table. "Because of the kids?"

She suddenly looked weary. It made him want to do everything he could to support her. "Partly, yes. Because when would I even have the time for a relationship? Any time not spent at the club is with my kids—it has to be."

"Of course," he agreed.

"My ex…" she started, then swallowed. "He needed a lot of attention. He liked me as a stay-at-home wife so I could be Mommy to him, too." She spread her hands. "But this is my dream. I've always wanted to own my own club. In the end, he made me choose."

Rick's eyebrows shot up. "Wow. Yeah, I can see why you wouldn't want to rush into any kind of relationship after that experience. Not all men are like that, though." He kicked himself. Why was he trying to convince her to date, when he couldn't date her? What? Did he want her to date someone else?

81

Oddly, he almost did. No, not someone else, but he wanted her to be happy, fulfilled. He wanted her to have a man willing to stand behind her and support her every step of the way. She deserved that.

He wished it could be him.

"Yeah, that's what my friends say," she said lightly. "But I still don't have time, so it's a moot point."

"Guess we'll have to settle for a booty call now and then."

Her lovely lips curved into a smile. "I guess so."

"I promise not to act like a dick the next time I see you in front of your kids."

She laughed that husky laugh that made his entire body supercharge. "Thank you. So did you really have anything you wanted to talk to me about for the Fostering Christmas event?"

"Yeah, I wanted to see what you think of my *Ho-ho-ho*." He pitched his voice deeper on the *ho-ho's*, attracting the curious stares from the people around them.

She slapped his forearm, laughing. "Stop it."

"Well, I also wondered if you're up for negotiating some naughty moments with Santa?"

She licked a bit of the lemon oil off her fingertip, taking her time and making eyes at him. Her lips puckered around her fingertip and his cock grew hard. "Hmm... that might be possible. After the kids have left, of course."

He shifted in his seat to adjust his cock. "I'll be looking forward to it." Actually he was looking forward to something sooner. Like another Saturday night closing hookup.

"Brandy, you're a breath of fresh air."

She lifted a brow. "How so?"

"You're mature." Gah—he bit his tongue when he realized he was insulting her. She probably had a few years on him. "I don't mean age-wise. I mean emotionally. It was so easy for us both to lay out our situations and find a resolution."

She pursed her lips, a flirty smile still on her face. "That's another reason I couldn't date you."

"Why?"

"Everyone would call me a cougar."

He rolled his eyes. "Oh please. You can't be much older than I am. And you look younger." He knocked his head with his fist. "You haven't been thrown to the ground too many times like I have."

She laughed and sat back in her seat. "Well, thanks. I don't believe in age, anyway." She waved her hand as if they were talking about fairies or invisibility cloaks.

Refreshing. As a professional ball player whose career had already ended, he could use a little of that philosophy himself. For a moment, the image of him growing old—or rather, not growing old with Brandy flashed in his mind. It was odd because he'd never pictured himself long-term with any woman, no matter what age or circumstance. What was it about this blonde vixen that made her seem so compatible?

Something in the center of his chest ached.

Too bad. In another life, she would be the one.

Chapter Seven

Brandy nibbled on her lip. It was Saturday night. They hadn't made a date, but she'd be surprised if Rick didn't show up. She'd told him it was the one night when she closed up and didn't have to run home to the kids. She honestly wasn't sure if she wanted him to come or not. Well, her body definitely wanted him to, but her brain kept screaming at her to pull back. This adventure wasn't going anywhere. Yes, it was good sex, but even that was a distraction from the things she ought to be doing—like planning for the grand openings of her new stores.

Even so, when one-half hour before closing, Rick's hulking form appeared in the doorway, her heart did a double backflip of joy. He carried his gym bag and was dressed in workout clothes—an old T-shirt stretched across his muscled chest.

All resistance disappeared when he stood in front of her. It was like her brain just checked out and her hormones took over. As proof, she tossed out a flirty smile. "Hey, Coach. You ready for your workout?"

He gave her an up-and-down sweep of his eyes. "Are you going to be my trainer?"

With her hands on her hips, she strolled around

the counter and gave him a mock-critical examination. "Yep, I can whip you into shape."

The corners of his lips lifted. "Show me what you got."

Hardly anyone was left in the place, but she refrained from acting on the urge to slap him on the ass the way football coaches do. They would get frisky soon enough.

They headed into the weight room.

"Let's start on the treadmill to warm up." She set a timer for him and walked around the club, checking to see how many people remained. She heard sounds from the men's locker room, and two women had just headed out of the women's room, leaving for the night. One lady was on a stationary bike and two guys were running around the track. She willed them all to leave. Pronto.

She ran Rick through the standard machines, dirty ideas about what they might do on each one crowding her brain. Despite the fact that he no longer played professional ball, he kept up his fitness as if he might be called back at any moment. Every muscle was defined, and he possessed a physical awareness she rarely witnessed. She didn't even pretend not to ogle him, her eyes tracing his abs, the powerful quads, and when he turned around, his perfect gluteus maximus.

Finally—*finally*—it appeared they were alone. She locked the front door after the last person left and switched off the lights in the main weight room, so they wouldn't be seen through the wall of windows.

"Is my workout over?" There was a suggestive lilt to his voice, the curve of his lips a sensual reminder of the commanding way he kissed.

"Oh no. Not hardly. Get on the row machine."

He hadn't even broken a sweat, yet, as far as she could tell. Not that she intended to provide him with a "real" workout. Or at least, she planned to get "real" with him in a different way. He sat down on it and gripped the handles while she adjusted the weights.

Then she sauntered back and straddled him.

His breath left in a whoosh, eyes darkening and going heavy-lidded. "Mmm, now this is the kind of workout I've been needing." His cock hardened against the heat of her sex.

She wiggled in place, rubbing her clit over the bulge in his gym shorts. She bit his ear. "Better start rowing," she murmured with sexy warning in her voice.

"Yes, ma'am." He pulled the handles hard, yanking them both forward, too fast.

She squealed and giggled, tightening her grip around his neck. His scent enthralled her, masculine and clean. "I lowered the weights since you're pulling me, too."

"That's good, I like playing Incredible Hulk." He showed off his manly strength while she rocked her pelvis over his growing cock. She wore only a pair of thin stretch pants without panties and the friction against his bulge had her wet in seconds. Her breasts ached, nipples hardened against the fabric of her yoga top.

He reached around and took the two handles in one fist, using the other to grip her ass and pull her even closer to his hips.

"Ah, ah," she scolded. "Both hands on the handles. I'm the trainer tonight."

He jumped and removed his hand, taking hold of the handle and rowing them even faster.

She held onto his neck, giggling at the ride.

She rather liked being in charge. Justin had never let her lead and before she'd met her ex, she'd been too young to even understand what a power exchange in sex play meant. As she considered what it meant for Rick to not use his hands, a wicked idea grew in her mind.

"Have you ever done TRX, Rick?"

"Hmm mm. But I've heard it's good. I'm just old school."

"I want to show you the TRX studio. Why don't you pop in the men's locker room and take a quick shower, then meet me in there?"

He hadn't caught on yet to what was in store in the TRX room, and the amiable if slightly puzzled expression on his face had her stifling a laugh. He picked up his gym bag, which they'd never bothered putting in the locker room and headed down the hall to the men's locker room.

While he showered, she grabbed a few things from her office and went into the TRX room. She flicked on the closet light, just to give the room an ambient glow. Ropes hung from hooks in the ceiling for suspension training.

Rick didn't make her wait long. Within a few minutes, he walked in wearing nothing but a towel around his waist, his muscled chest still glistening with moisture.

Yum. She wouldn't mind looking at that sight every day for the rest of her life.

She walked over to one set of ropes and stood beneath it. "Okay, I need you to stand right here."

He ambled over, the curious but game little smile still tugging at his lips.

I so love this guy.

Wait—where did that thought come from? *Love* and *Rick* should not be considered in the same sentence. This was a booty call. A hookup. Nothing more.

"Now hold your arms over your head."

His smile was lascivious. Hungry. Thrilled. He held her eyes and slowly reached his arms over his head.

Aaaand, she couldn't reach. Because he was hella tall.

"Hang on just a second," she breathed and ran to the closet for one of the stools used in step class.

Rick was laughing when she returned and this time she did swat his ass, which caused his towel to drop. His cock jutted out, thick and long, a drop of pre-cum glistening on the slit.

A flush of heat spread across her chest.

"Oopsy!" she sang with mock chagrin.

She set the step next to him and climbed on it to wrap his wrists with the TRX ropes. Obviously, it would be easy for him to extricate himself, but that wasn't the point. This was play.

"How's that?" She tugged the knots tight.

His gaze glittered and his eyes never moved from her face. "Elevating," he joked.

She smacked his ass again. It was solid muscle, so it probably hurt her hand more than him.

She trailed a hand over his beautiful torso. It felt so delicious to be in charge. Of course her beautiful lover could overpower her in a flash—he was bigger and stronger than her in every way. But that wasn't the point. He was willing to let her lead tonight and he looked as excited and thrilled as she was.

With her hands molded to his glorious pecs, she licked a long line up the center of his torso, savoring the taste of his skin.

His breath shortened, gaze grew hungry. She pulled out the tube of Tiger Balm sports rub she had grabbed from her office and unscrewed the cap. Squeezing a bit on her finger, she swirled it over one of his nipples, squeezing as it grew stiff. She gave the same treatment to the other one, then blew lightly on them.

"How's that?" Her voice sounded husky.

His cock bobbed, beckoning her.

"Tingly."

She blew on his nipples again, knowing the cool prickling sensations would only increase over the next half hour.

"And for your cock…"

Alarm crossed his face and she laughed. "No, not the Tiger Balm. For your cock, I brought a breath mint."

She unwrapped it and popped it in her mouth, using her tongue to move it all around. "Ready?"

"God, yes," he groaned.

* * *

Nothing could be lovelier than the sight of Brandy dropping to her knees and parting those luscious lips of hers to take his cock in her mouth.

"A-a-a-ah," he exhaled as her hot, wet mouth engulfed his throbbing cock.

She gripped the base of his member and took the rest of him deep into her throat, her tongue swirling around his staff.

He wanted to reach for her head, to pet her, or encourage, but his wrists were tied. Which was the point, he supposed. This was her show. And damn, if she didn't know how to play it.

She pulled all the way off, letting the coolness of the mint and the air stimulate his moistened cock. The outside of his cock felt frosted with an arctic chill while the inside pulsed with heat.

He groaned.

Her little pink tongue extended and she licked around the head of his cock. Once more she sheathed his entire cock in her mouth, coating it with her minty fresh tongue.

He shuddered with pleasure.

Working both her fist and her mouth, she glided in and out over his manhood. Her fist squeezed tight at the base and pushed and pulled to follow her mouth, making it seem like she had him all the way to the very base of his cock.

She sucked hard, hollowing her cheeks and increasing her pace.

His thighs tensed, balls tightened. Just as he nearly reached nirvana, she pulled off again and blew.

"Ugn." He thrust his hips in the direction of her mouth like the needy bastard he'd become.

"How's the mint?"

He shuddered with pleasure just at the mention of it. "Frosty." His voice sounded gravelly.

She gripped his cock in both hands, interlacing her fingers and squeezing hard.

"Oh God, yes," he grunted, hips snapping.

Her lips stretched into a wicked smile. "More?"

"Yes, please."

"Well, since you asked so nicely..." This time she gripped his ass cheeks, letting him feel her nails as she took him deep into her throat.

He tensed, his breath coming in pants, his cock in glorious ecstasy. Each caress of her tongue sent fresh shots of lust kicking through him. Each time she deep-throated, his eyes rolled back in his head and a rumble sounded in his throat.

"Brandy... " he growled. His balls tightened. "I'm going to come."

She sucked harder. Apparently Brandy wasn't afraid to swallow.

His thighs flexed and cum shot down his shaft.

"Oh God..." He shot his load.

Brandy continued sucking, continued gliding over his cock, taking in his seed. She sat back and swallowed, a satisfied smile curving her beautiful lips. "How'd I do, Coach?"

He sagged, letting his body hang from the ropes. "Incredible."

She stood on the little step stool she'd brought over and untied the ropes.

The moment he was free, he gathered her up into his arms and kissed her. Her mouth was hot and he tasted the salty remnants of his cum on her tongue, along with the spice of the now-dissolved mint. "You are incredible. That was incredible." His brain couldn't seem to make his mouth say anything more intelligent.

He kneaded her ass, pulling her hips up against him and wedging a knee between her thighs. Her cheeks fit perfectly in his large palms and he loved the firmness of her muscular buns. "Is it my turn now?"

Her pussy wept through her stretch pants, dampening his thigh as he rubbed her clit against his leg.

She reached up and brushed his shaggy bangs out of his eyes. "What did you have in mind?"

"Come here." He picked her up so she straddled him and he carried her back into the weight room, where he set her down on the abs bench. "Reach for the handles," he murmured and pushed her torso until she lay on her back.

She obeyed, and he stripped off her pants in seconds flat. She'd groomed for him. Last week, her pussy had been trimmed to a neat landing strip. This week, she'd shaved it completely bare.

"Oh, that's hot," he rumbled, pushing her knees back toward her chest. "Did you groom for me?" He shouldn't ask a question like that. They weren't dating and they certainly weren't exclusive, but he felt extremely possessive of that beautiful little pussy at the moment.

"Yes." Her perfectly flat belly fluttered.

He straddled the bench below her hips and lowered his head, licking into her dewy folds. "Mmm," he said when she gasped. "I've been imagining this all week long."

She looked porn-perfect, lying back on the table, her toned body lithe and ultra-feminine. So perfect, in fact, that he just had to get her top off for the full effect.

He tugged it off over her head and then stood back to survey her. "Absolutely beautiful."

She lifted her hips in a clear invitation.

Damn—even though she'd just sucked him off, his cock wanted to go for full penetration. But he wasn't sure they were ready for that and he didn't want to go get a condom out of his bag. Instead, he returned to his position between her legs. Holding her thighs apart, he lowered his head and licked along the seam of her sex. Her clit hardened under the application of his tongue and he sucked it until she cried out, lifting her hips from the table. He pressed them back down and rolled her knees back toward her shoulders.

Good thing she was so flexible.

He licked her from anus to clit and back again, making her moan and squeal.

"Rick... Rick... oh God, don't stop," she wailed.

He slid two fingers into her and curled them, caressing her inner wall, seeking her g-spot. He found it. A button of tissue tightened and firmed under his touch and Brandy let out a plaintive wail.

He pumped his fingers in and out of her as he sucked her clit.

Her strong thighs clamped around his ears, pressing in.

He added a third finger and shoved deeper, harder, faster.

"Oh pleeeease, oh please, oh... oh!"

She squirted as she came. He'd never made a woman squirt before and somehow it seemed perfect that it had been with Brandy, the woman who had blown his already decent sex life out of the water. Talk about porn perfect.

Her internal muscles squeezed his fingers,

making him wish, once more, it had been his cock inside her.

Next time.

If there was a next time. Yes, there would be a next time if he had anything to do with it.

He waited until all the ripples of orgasm had quieted and she went limp, then eased his fingers out and used his towel to help her clean up.

Because she looked too dazed to move, he slid an arm under her shoulders and lifted her up, first to sit, then slowly to stand.

She leaned against him, her knees wobbly.

He loved the feel of her, loved taking her weight. He wished she'd lean on him more. He gripped her nape and moved her long, straight blond off her shoulder to kiss there.

"I'm going to shower," she murmured.

"I'll wipe down the equipment," he offered. He gave her ass a slap as she teetered away, loving the sound of flesh smacking flesh.

She looked over her shoulder with a seductive smile and his pulse quickened.

She had enjoyed it as much as he had. God, he really hoped this wasn't their last time. Even though it couldn't go anywhere. He had to tell himself that last part firmly, because some part of him already wanted to pick out wallpaper with her.

But no. No go. Brandy Love wasn't "the one."

Too bad.

Chapter Eight

Brandy and her 11-year-old Claire were out shopping. It was one of the greatest pleasures of having a daughter, in her opinion. Lots of women shuddered at the idea of encouraging their daughters' inner shopper for fear they'd be set up for years of heavy expenditures, but not her.

Claire was the perfect companion. She helped Brandy hunt down the right sizes—which was hard for a slender, 5'9" woman—and came into the dressing room to give her opinion. Claire, herself, wasn't overly fussy with clothes, which meant Brandy still got to pick them for her. Yes, she'd been blessed with 11 years of dressing up her own beautiful baby doll.

Going clothes shopping three weeks before Christmas probably wasn't her best move, but she wanted a new outfit for the Fostering Christmas event. The mall was packed with wild-eyed shoppers who must be either panicked to find the right gift, or freaking out about how much they'd spent. And yeah, if the relentless Christmas songs hadn't been enough at the gym, they were driving her nuts now.

Her cell phone rang while she was in the middle of changing into a pair of slacks. "Will you grab that for me?" she asked Claire.

Her daughter dug in her purse and pulled it out. "It says Coach Morehouse."

She frowned. Rick was calling? In the middle of the football clinic? Cold tendrils of fear snaked around her heart and she snatched the phone out of her daughter's grasp. "Hello? Rick? What's up?"

"I'm sorry, Brandy, but there's been an accident."

Her heart shot up to her throat, choking her breath.

The words no mother ever wants to hear.

She forced an exhale and sank to the bench in the dressing room. "Tell me."

"Sam's okay, but it looks like he may have fractured his arm. I'm going to take him to the hospital myself, unless you prefer I call an ambulance."

"No, I want you to take him. Which one?"

"Houston Memorial."

She closed her eyes and drew a breath to the count of four, forcing oxygen in. "We'll meet you there. Have you called his father?"

"No, do you want to?"

Not really, but someone had to. "Yes, I'll call him. See you there."

She hit end, her heart pattering against her ribs with an unnatural beat.

"Come on, we have to go. Your brother broke his arm."

"Oh no," Claire exclaimed, digging through the castoff clothes for Brandy's pants. "Here mom."

She shucked the try-on clothes and pulled on her pants. Claire held her purse out for her and she caught it on her arm as they swooped out of the dressing room. Cold chills continued to pour through her body, even as she counseled herself, *Just a broken arm. Not life threatening.*

After fumbling for her phone, she dialed Justin.

"What's up," he answered curtly.

"Sam may have broken his arm. They're taking him to Houston Memorial now."

"What? Jesus! Who's *they*?"

"Coach Morehouse."

"Are you kidding me? They should have called an ambulance. He will totally be liable if anything happens to Sam during transport."

"Shut up, Justin." Always the lawyer—he drove her freaking nuts. Everything was about a lawsuit. "I authorized him to take Sam." Seriously, if it had been in an ambulance, then Justin would've complained about the expense. He just liked to poke holes in any decision she ever made.

She ended the call before she said something she'd regret and focused on finding the fastest route to the hospital. Once there, she rushed into the waiting room, to find Sam and Rick sitting in the chairs. Rick's hand rested on Sam's shoulder and Sam's face was pinched up tight.

"Sam, baby." She rushed over, her stomach clenching at the ghostly pallor of his face. "Did they give him anything for the pain?" she asked Rick.

Rick shook his head. His jaw was tight as if he, too, suffered right along with Sam. "I should have demanded some. I'm sorry."

She dug in her purse for some ibuprofen. It would be better if Sam took something before they did the X-rays. She remembered when Claire had broken her tibia as a kindergartener, they didn't give her anything until after and she'd screamed bloody murder every time they moved her during the X-rays. She handed him three ibuprofen. "Here, take these."

Sam grimaced, because swallowing pills wasn't his forte yet, but he took a big swig from his water bottle and got them down.

"Samuel Anderson?" A nurse called from the door to the E.R. "Come on back, and we'll get you X-rayed now."

All four of them stood and came forward, Sam wincing with each step he took, the jostling obviously paining him. When they reached the door, the nurse shook her head and pointed at Claire. "She can't come back."

Brandy heaved a bitter sigh. *Really? What in the hell did they expect a mother of more than one child to do?*

"I'll stay with her," Rick offered.

Claire's eyes were large and round.

"Claire, this is Rick, Sam's coach. He's super nice. Are you okay staying with him in the waiting room? You can just watch TV or something?"

Claire nodded, although she saw the doubt scrawled across her face. But of course, she couldn't protest. Obviously Brandy needed to be with Sam.

"When Daddy gets here, I'll bet he'll stay with you, okay, hon?" Even as she said the words, she doubted they were true. Justin wouldn't be selfless enough to sit with Claire, he'd have to be back there with Sam making sure everything was going just the way he thought it should go.

She went back with Sam, trying to distract him from the pain of having the bones moved and arranged for the X-rays. "When your sister broke her leg, she screamed bloody murder back here."

Sam forced a smile, but his teeth were still gritted. "Oh yeah?"

"Yeah. She was in her tights and leotard, so everyone kept stopping and saying "Ohhhh, what happened to the little ballerina?"

Sam smiled again. "Where was I?"

"You were still at soccer practice. Meg took you home and kept you there until we were out."

"Where was Dad?"

Where indeed? He'd stayed at work and left her to handle it. He trusted her decisions then. When they were married. It was only now that he had to show up and demand his vote in every decision. 'I don't remember," she murmured.

They took the last X-ray and put him in a wheelchair to take into an exam room. Justin showed up as they headed in.

"How was Claire doing out there?"

Justin gave a surly shrugged. "Why is that coach still here?"

"He offered to stay with Claire, since she's not allowed in here." *Something you should be doing.*

Justin paced the small room. Sam picked up the remote and flipped through the channels on the television.

"Has the doctor been in?" Justin asked.

"No, not yet."

"Do they think he'll need surgery?"

"I'm not sure," she said with exaggerated calm. "Like I said, the doctor hasn't been in yet. I'm going to go check on Claire if you're going to stay here." Really, she needed some breathing space.

She walked out to the waiting room and found Claire and Rick both huddled over Rick's phone, which was in Claire's hands. She was playing some sort of game while he coached over her shoulder.

"Get that one, over there, over there, over there," he whispered urgently, pointing at the screen.

Her body leaned to the right and she stamped her feet, then sagged. "Ugh. I died."

"Hey guys." Despite the stress of the situation, a smile crept to her lips. "I see you're staying entertained."

"Yeah, mom. Rick has this great game. Can we download it on your phone?"

"Sure." She sank into the chair next to Rick. She should've sat beside Claire, but she needed Rick's strength, needed someone to be strong for her for once.

He put his arm on the back of her chair, barely touching her shoulder, but she sensed he support nonetheless. "How's he doing?"

She sighed. "It's hurting him a lot. We're hoping he won't need surgery. So what happened? Did he get tackled?"

Rick nodded. "Yes. He got thrown into the air and landed on it. He's a tough kid, though, not that I would've blamed him for blubbering his eyes out."

Some buzzing, anxious tension in her solar plexus settled down. Rick did that to her. She could relax with him.

"Thanks for staying with Claire," she said softly.

Claire had already started up a new game and didn't appear to be listening, anyway.

"My pleasure. She's a good egg."

Nope, Claire wasn't listening—she didn't react to that at all.

Stress made Brandy weak—she leaned her shoulder against his.

He stroked her opposite shoulder. "How are you doing, Mama Bear?"

She let out a shaky breath. "Okay. I had to get away from Justin. Get a little space." She wanted to say more, but not in front of Claire.

His fingers found the nape of her neck underneath her hair, and he stroked the back of his thumb lazily up and down, soothing her.

Another coil in her belly unwound.

"I should probably go back in there. Listen, if you don't want to stay—"

Rick held up his hand. "I'm staying," he said firmly.

She exhaled. "Thanks. So much. This means a lot to me."

Her knees wobbled when she stood. She took one more glance over her shoulder as she headed back in. Rick was already leaning back over Claire, actively participating in the game with her.

God, what a dream man.

Her chest ached just a little. She wanted him. For real—not just for booty calls.

Too bad it couldn't be.

Because in another life, he'd be the one.

* * *

Brandy's ex walked out first. He saw Rick notice him, but he didn't acknowledge him, just put on his sunglasses and walked out the door. He didn't even say goodbye to his own daughter.

Jackass.

He shouldn't judge. He might be bitter if he'd lost Brandy as his wife, too. She was a force to be reckoned with. She ushered Sam out a few minutes later. Sam wore a bright green cast on his arm and a little of the color had returned to his face.

"Come on, Claire-bear, they're out," he said. The endearment had just slipped off his tongue, and he immediately regretted it. For one thing, she was too old to be called names like that. For another, he wasn't supposed to be getting into a relationship with these kids.

She handed his phone to him with a smile that wrenched his heart. Pure sweetness. What a beautiful kid. If he was her dad, he'd get a bat to keep the boys away from her, because in a year or two she'd be breaking hearts left and right.

"My mom calls me that," she said.

His heart stuttered again. "Does she?" Did his voice waver?

They walked over to meet Brandy and Sam. He tousled Sam's hair. "How's the arm now, champ?"

"Better now that the cast is on it. You were right."

Rick had told him on the drive over that the worst was the movement and instability of the bone.

"Well, it could be the painkillers kicking in, too." He smiled.

They walked outside and Brandy looked around, a lost look on her face.

"Where are you parked?" He touched her lower back to let her know he was still there to help.

"I... honestly can't remember. I was so worried when I got here..."

Claire pointed. "It's over there, Mom. Remember? We walked past that sign."

Brandy gave a sheepish grin. He doubted she often lost focus or forget things. "Where are you parked?" she asked.

He jerked his thumb in the opposite direction. "That way, but I'll walk you to your car."

He expected her to protest, but her unbreakable facade had cracked this afternoon. "Thanks." Her voice was soft, the gaze she sent him, sweet.

His heart tumbled around in his chest. Lord help him but he wanted to receive a thousand more of those. He wanted to earn that look a hundred times a day until he died. He struggled to compose himself, to pull his thoughts together.

"You take it easy, Sam. I'd still like to see you at the clinic for the last session, even if you can't play. Injured players still stick with their team, you know."

He wasn't sure if that suggestion would meet with resistance or not, but Sam's smile looked enthusiastic. "Yeah, okay. I'll be there." They reached the car. "Coach..." Sam scuffed the toe of his sneaker against the other shoe. "What does this do to my chances—"

"You're on the team, kid."

Both Brandy and Sam jerked their heads up, their matching blue eyes wide with surprise.

"Really?"

He dropped a hand on his shoulder. "Yes. From what I saw, you're a hard worker and you have a great arm. With a little more skill-building and team-work, you could become a star player by the time you're a senior."

103

Sam's jaw dropped. "Are you serious?" He looked over at his mother, who beamed back and winked.

"I'm dead serious. I'd like to have you on the team next year. JV to start, but I wouldn't be surprised if you were on the varsity team by your sophomore year."

He looked thrilled, then suddenly, his face fell. "Mom, what about what Dad said?"

Brandy tensed. "I'll deal with your father."

"What did he say?" Yeah, it wasn't any of his business, but he already cared what happened in this family, already felt like he played a role here.

"He said no more football. That it's too dangerous."

He struggled to keep his cool. He answered this objection with parents all the time. For some reason, though, this time it pissed him off. "Football is a dangerous sport, yes. But they are doing their best to regulate it to avoid serious injuries. What happened to you today... " -he rubbed his face, searching for a good way to rationalize it- "it doesn't mean it will happen again. You can't live your life in fear of getting hurt, nor can you beat yourself up when you do. The point is to believe you can always recover from it, you can always come back."

Sam looked at him doubtfully. "But you didn't come back from your injury."

"Sure I did. I'm coaching you. This is my life's work—this is what makes me happiest. I liked playing professional ball, but it was only half as satisfying as coaching. And I'm dead serious about that."

Brandy's eyes brightened with tears. Some of

Sam's skepticism had disappeared and he looked hopeful again.

"You just worry about your recovery, and let your mom and I worry about convincing your dad."

Your mom and I.

Had he seriously just used those words together in the same sentence? Was he already considering them as a team that worked together for the good of the kids? Something deep inside him shifted, and the discomfort of it had him ready to run for the hills.

He touched Brandy's shoulder. "I'll give you a call tomorrow to check on him," he said. "On all of you." He glanced at Claire, who smiled shyly.

"Take care. All of you."

He walked away, his heart pounding, a tingle running over his skin.

What in the hell was he doing?

Chapter Nine

True to his word, Rick checked in the next day. Only he didn't call. He texted, *Bringing pizza over for dinner. How's the patient?*

Her heart flip flopped like a fish on land. He was coming over. *Here*. To her house. With pizza. It was not a booty call. It wasn't even a date. It was like... a relationship.

No, that wasn't right. He was Sam's coach and Sam had been injured on his watch. Of course that's all this was. Because he'd already made it crystal clear he wouldn't date a single mom.

She shouldn't read anything more into this—Rick was just an awesome guy who cared a lot about the kids he coached. Maybe this was why he was so afraid of dating a single mom. He adored kids so much, he knew he'd fall in love. Well, her kids sure loved him right back.

She could argue that they'd only just met, and that could wear off, but she didn't think it would. They liked Rick because he was genuine and a good person. He radiated tenderness, comfort, love, strength. They wouldn't put it into those words, but that was who he was. An amazing, stand up guy.

106

Who also happened to be six feet five inches of solid muscle and hunky good looks. A man who made her knees go weak with just a smile. A man who'd let her tie him up and ride him on the row machine.

Her toes curled just remembering their last steamy night together. She wanted a repeat, soon. Except... maybe this was getting to be too much. Too often. Too intimate. For two people not in a relationship. She sighed, the giddy angst that had been eating at her since the day she met Rick ratcheting up again.

Rick showed up at dinnertime with a giant pizza—half pepperoni, half sausage and jalapeno. He walked in like he owned the place—no, he was respectful, but he also seemed perfectly comfortable in her house. She liked it. He tossed the pizza in the middle of the table and said, "have at it, kids."

The kids scrambled up from the couch and came over, digging in. Sam had stayed home from school that day, and his arm still hurt quite a bit, but his mood was totally back to normal. She'd worked from home to keep an eye on him.

Rick chuckled at the exuberance with which the kids attacked the food. It looked like she never fed them. "I went to college with this guy who had moved here from Egypt when he was 12. He said the first time he saw the way Americans ate pizza he was shocked."

Claire giggled, her mouth already stuffed full.

"He said it seemed sort of representative of our country as a whole—everyone scrambling to get as many pieces as they can before it's gone."

"That's a weird story," Sam said while chewing.

Rick handed her a plastic bag with two styrofoam containers. "Here's the salad to go with it."

She smiled. Thoughtful. He probably suspected she didn't like to stuff herself with too many carbs, not that she was going to resist a piece of sausage jalapeno. Yum. She got out four plates and served the salad.

"So how's the arm, man?" Rick asked Sam.

Sam bobbed his head, now stuffing the second slice of pizza in his face. "Good. Better."

"He sees the orthopedist tomorrow. Then we find out if he needs surgery or not."

"Fingers crossed you don't. But either way, it will be six to eight weeks in a cast, but then you'll be good as new." He directed his attention to Claire. "How about you, missy? Do you have any homework?"

"I already did it."

She nearly swooned. Had he actually just asked her kid if her homework was done?

"Good, because I brought over some movies. I'm sure you've already seen it, but I rented the new *Star Wars* movie. And how about *Jurassic World*?"

"Yes, I love that one," Claire exclaimed.

"Which one?"

"Well, both, but *Jurassic World* is my favorite. It's so good."

"How about you, Sam?"

Sam shrugged. "Either one. I like them both."

Rick tossed them to Sam. "Let's get it started then," he swiveled to her, "if that's okay with Mom, that is."

She nodded, hoping she didn't appear as starry eyed as she felt at the moment. Really, she shouldn't be more excited about a man giving her children attention than she was about him... well, doing naughty things to her, but it might be an even tie.

* * *

Rick sat on the couch next to Brandy and Claire. Sam had curled up in the Lazy-boy chair. As Rick twirled a strand of Brandy's cornsilk hair between his fingers, he realized he was in too deep. He'd known it at the hospital, and he definitely knew it when he made the choice to visit them here at their home. He'd met the kids. He liked the kids—a lot. And he liked the way Brandy went soft when he interacted with them, watching him with those big baby blues as if he were some kind of hero.

Yeah, he wanted to be her hero.

But that was messed up. He didn't get involved with a woman with kids. They were already warming up to him, already trusting him. What would happen if he and Brandy... what? Called it quits? They weren't even together yet. Strange, how he considered they were.

Claire passed the popcorn down to him and he scooped a handful and handed the bowl back. This was comfortable. Strangely, he felt almost more at home here than he did in his own bachelor pad.

Was this what had been missing in his life? Family? Kids? He'd never known he wanted them. He got plenty of kid interaction coaching—more than enough. Why, then, did he care so much about hanging out here with Claire and Sam? Because they belonged to Brandy?

Or because Brandy and her kids just *fit* with him?

He found himself imagining bringing them all over to his mom's house—the one he'd bought her when he'd received his first pro paycheck. His mom would love the kids. And she'd adore Brandy, too. They were similar in many ways—classy, graceful, socially adept. Caring.

The movie ended and he uncrossed his long legs and reluctantly pushed himself up to stand, turning to offer his hand to Brandy. "Well, it must be your bedtime, kids. I'll see you later. Sam, I hope to see you at the clinic on Sunday. Tell me if you want help talking to your dad."

Sam bobbed his head. "Yeah, thanks, okay."

"Good night, Claire-Bear."

She jumped off the couch and wrapped her arms around his waist.

For a moment, he lost his breath.

"Good night, Coach."

He kissed the top of her head. "Good night, squirt."

Brandy walked him to the door and stepped out onto the porch, shutting the door behind her. "Thanks for this. It was really sweet of you."

He loved the way she looked up at him—the tough-as-nails Houston entrepreneur had turned yielding. He gripped the back of her head and brushed his lips across hers—softly at first, then claiming them with more force, licking into her mouth. She opened for him, leaned her incredible body against his and kissed him back, twisting her lips over his.

His pulse quickened, a shot of lust kicking through him. But no—God, no. Her kids were right inside, probably wondering what in the hell they were doing. They broke apart.

"When can I see you?" he found himself asking without his brain even knowing he was going to do it. And damned if he didn't want a real date with her—not just a hookup. Although he wouldn't be upset about a hookup, either.

"I'm not sure. I have the kids all week."

"How about lunch?" Yep, definitely a date.

She arched a brow. "But we aren't dating."

He shrugged. "So? How about lunch?"

The edges of her mouth curved into the sexy suggestion of a smile. "Okay, lunch. Wednesday?"

"I'll pick you up at the club. Noon?"

She nodded, smiling. "Sounds good."

He snaked an arm around her waist and pulled her against him, sampling her lips once more. "Good night." He released her, tipped an imaginary hat, and headed down the sidewalk.

"Good night." She sounded breathless.

He did that to her. His chest swelled.

Crap, he was totally in too deep.

* * *

By Wednesday, she'd thought herself into a rut about Rick. What was the deal? He said he couldn't do a relationship because she had kids, but then he'd dropped by her house and cozied up to Sam and Claire. And what was this lunch date thing? *They weren't dating.*

Now he was taking up way too much headspace. She'd said she didn't have time for a relationship but

111

she'd been thinking about Rick all week. Sometimes fantasizing about more shower sex, sometimes about *more*. About having Rick in her life—what it would be like to see more of him, to wake up beside him, or fall asleep next to him. To share more of the everyday life moments like pizza and a movie. That was the part that scared her. Rick was giving off mixed messages, and she didn't have time in her life to get jerked around. If they were going to have hot sex, that was fine, but she needed to draw firm boundaries.

She texted him that morning. *Let's make it a nooner. My house is free.*

There. Just sex.

He responded immediately, *Sounds like a perfect plan to me. Meet you there.*

Her pulse quickened. She headed to the women's locker room and took another shower. She'd only taught one class and had hardly broken a sweat, but she wanted to be fresh and clean for Rick. After grabbing her purse, she headed out.

As she climbed in her car, another text from Rick came through. *We'll drop your car at the shop on the way back. I made an appointment for your power steering.*

She blinked. Then blinked again. Seriously? Was this guy for real? That's pretty presumptuous. She didn't need anyone to run her life. She'd worked hard to earn her independence from Justin. She sure wasn't going to let her booty call step in and start running the show. What? He didn't think she could get it done on her own? Because car mechanics are something only *men* can handle?

Before she should reply, he sent another one. *It*

will take three hours and I can drive you back to get it when it's done. Checked your teaching schedule online. Should be okay?

Grr. Yes, it was really nice of him, but she hadn't asked for help. Booty calls don't step in and get your car fixed. She'd have to have a talk with him about this.

She texted back, *No, thanks. I can take care of it,* and started her car.

He responded with a series of question marks, which she ignored.

She parked in her driveway. It seemed so naughty to be home in the middle of the day. Like ditching class in high school, only naughtier, because it was to have sex.

She pulled open the dresser drawer that held her lingerie, wondering what kind Rick liked. Flowy see-through top? Nah... Thigh highs with the seam down the back? Hmm, yes, maybe. And what on top? Bra? Or corset? She decided on black lacy bra, black panties and the lace-topped thigh-highs with the seam down the back. Oh, and high heels. Because Rick Morehouse was tall enough to top her height no matter how high the shoes.

She traipsed around the house—yes, in the full get up and heels—and straightened up. The kids had left jackets and shoes strewn about. Papers from school piled on her kitchen counter.

A tap sounded at the door.

"Come in," she called.

The door slid open and...

Oh God, no. *"Mom!"*

Her mother took one look at her and gasped. "Brandy-Marie, what on Earth?"

113

"None of your business, mom." She sounded more snappish than she meant to. She needed to get rid of her mom before Rick got there and... ugh. She really didn't want to explain this to her mother.

She hustled into the bedroom and pulled a robe on. "Mom, why are you here?" she called out.

"Well I saw your car in the driveway and I was afraid Sam was still home with his broken arm or something. I was going to tell you I would stay with him so you could go to work."

She emerged, tying the robe. "That's sweet, mom, but Sam's at school."

"I should hope so! What's going on? You don't have a date with Justin do you?"

"Justin? Mom, we're divorced."

"Well that doesn't mean you can't get back together."

Seriously? Her mom was worse than the kids.

"Mom, you gotta go. You're a total mood kill. I'll call you later, okay?"

Her mother wore a bewildered expression. "Well, okay, honey. Er... have fun!" She reached back through the door and waved as she left.

Brandy rolled her eyes and started to giggle.

* * *

Rick knocked on Brandy's door. He wasn't sure why she'd shot down his plan to have her car fixed, but the prospect of a nooner had his cock aching already.

She opened the door wearing... *gulp*. Holy shit. Brandy stepped back to let him in. She stood in three-inch heels and... damn. She ought to be working for

Victoria's Secret because he had *never* seen lingerie look so good on a woman. Her apple-sized breasts spilled out of a lacy black bra. Matching black panties and his favorite—thigh highs—completed the ensemble. Her long blond hair draped across one shoulder.

He shut the door and whistled. "You might need to bring me smelling salts."

She laughed—a husky, sexy sound that went straight to his cock.

"Are you hungry? Thirsty?"

He shook his head slowly. "Only for you."

"We need to have a little talk about your plans for my car." She reached out and hooked a finger behind one of the buttons of his shirt, using it to lead him behind her as she strutted down the hall, her heels clacking on the hardwood floors. He would never think of hardwood floors the same again. Or high heels. Or thigh highs.

What had she said? Plans for his car? He shook his head, trying to get some of the blood that had traveled two feet south back to his brain. "What's the problem?"

"The problem, *Coach*—" She flicked one of the buttons on his shirt open as they walked, so he moved to help her, unbuttoning from the bottom. "Is that we're not even dating. You're not my boyfriend or my husband. And I can handle these things on my own."

They reached the bedroom and his shirt now hung open. She spun around and her hands found his chest, fingernails scraping lightly through the light curls there. He couldn't concentrate on her words, which didn't seem to match her actions. Was she picking a fight? Or was this foreplay?

Hell, he didn't mind. Either way, he liked it.

"Never liked hair on a man's chest until I met you," she murmured, her voice dripping with that honey that made her sound so damn kissable.

Not wasting any time, he cupped her nape and pulled her in for a kiss, sucking her lower lip into his mouth and nipping.

"So you're mad? I was just trying to help."

"It was too much." She pressed her pert breasts up against his chest, yanking his shirt down off his arms as they kissed.

She was too much.

He ran his hands up and down her body, savoring the incredible softness of her bare skin, the toned muscles underneath and the freakin' beautiful wrappings she'd put herself in.

She started to pull the straps down off her bra, but he stopped her.

"No, don't," he said between kisses, backing her toward the bed. "I'm enjoying this outfit of yours way too much. Do not take anything off. Not even the heels." He used a stern voice.

Her nose scrunched up in an adorable way. "I thought I was leading here."

He flashed a wicked smile. "We just switched." He picked her up by the waist and plopped her on the bed on her back. "You got a problem with that?"

"Nope," she answered quickly, her eyes heavy-lidded with desire.

With a loose hold on her ankles, he lifted her legs straight up and spread them wide. "Show me that world-famous flexibility, baby. I want you to keep your legs just like this."

Her huge blue eyes watched him as he lowered to his knees and yanked the gusset of her panties to the side. Her pussy visibly clenched, the muscles lifting, quivering in anticipation of his mouth.

"I haven't stopped dreaming of this pussy since Saturday," he growled before he licked into her.

She shrieked and reached for his head, her pelvis lifting to meet him.

He licked a long, slow line up her sex, parting her labia and retracting her clitoral hood with the tip of his tongue.

She jerked beneath him, gasping, and her fingers wove into his hair.

He circled her clit, tracing it, then sucked the stiffened nubbin into his mouth.

"Oh God," Brandy moaned. "That tongue of yours…"

"Mm hm," he hummed against her flesh, licking up and down again at a faster rate.

"Whoa... .wow... wha-uh. Oh Jesus."

He screwed one finger inside her, continuing to flick her clit with his tongue.

"Rick," she panted, the breathy quality of her voice telling him how close she was to coming. "I want you inside me this time... please?"

Holy baby Jesus. He couldn't say no to that. With a pump of his finger inside her, he stood up.

"Oh yes," she said in anticipation. Her big baby doll eyes were glassy, pupils dilated with desire.

He yanked a condom out of his pocket and dropped his pants and boxer briefs to the floor, stepping out of them at the same time he ripped open the foil wrapper.

"Now, Rick," she moaned, as if her fuse had been lit and he needed to get inside her before the bomb went off.

Cock sheathed, he positioned himself between her legs, then changed his mind. "Roll over," he commanded.

She scrambled to comply, flipping her body so her high heels came to the floor as she bent over the side of the bed, leaning on her elbows

Damn... those thigh highs! Black seams charged up the backs of her stockings. She looked So. Incredibly. Beautiful.

She reached back and started to drag her panties down but he stopped her with a light slap on the ass.

"I said the outfit stays. Now spread your legs."

She moaned and moved her high heels farther apart. "Hurry, Rick."

His palms rounded circles over her ass and his eyes nearly rolled back in his head. How firm yet soft and yielding. He shoved her panties to the side and rubbed the head of his cock over her dewy-wet slit, then pushed in.

Her pussy opened for him, hot and welcoming.

Now it was his turn to groan. "You feel so good," he growled, taking several long, slow strokes in and out.

"Rick." Her voice had risen in pitch, the desperation to climax upon her.

He gripped her hips and gave it to her hard, bumping in and out.

"Yes," she moaned. "Yes, *please*, that's it!"

He drove harder, deeper, relishing the way her moist heat engulfed him.

Her breasts bobbed and swung as he bumped her from behind, the graceful slope of her sinuous back responding to each thrust. Her fingers twisted into the bedcovers and she dropped her cheek to the bed, eyes wide, mouth open and panting.

His thighs flexed, his own climax rushing nearer. He reached around the front of her and stuck his hand down her panties in the front. The moment he rubbed her clitoral hood over her pleasure center, she shattered. She screamed into the bedspread, hips bucking. Her muscles clamped down on his cock, squeezing.

He shoved in deep and stayed, still rubbing her clit from the front. Cum shot down his shaft. Her contracting muscles milked it from him, and his orgasm seemed to go on and on until he'd filled the condom. With one arm wrapped around her waist, he dropped his torso over hers, kissing her neck and shoulder.

"You are incredible," he murmured.

"And you are a superstar." She sounded contented, almost sleepy.

He could use a little post-sex nap himself. He eased off her and went to the bathroom to clean up.

When he returned, she still lay in the same position. He longed to pull her all the way up and lay down with her, but she'd been pretty clear about boundaries. Post-coital snuggling definitely wasn't been part of the booty-call plan. And she hadn't accepted his help with her car, which was also a signal.

He ought to be glad she was sticking to her refusal to enter a relationship, but something deep inside his chest began to ache as he pulled on his clothes.

This didn't feel right. Not at all.

She pushed herself up and glanced at the clock. "Ugh. I have to get back to the gym."

"I won't hold you up." He went in for a brief peck on the lips. "Thanks."

"Thank *you.*"

He pointed a finger at her. "You take care of that power steering."

She rolled her eyes and tossed the thigh-high she'd just pulled off at him. "Get out, you."

He chuckled. "Leaving."

Well, that had been pretty clear. This was just sex. That shouldn't irritate him as much as it did.

* * *

"So there I am in my full Fredericks of Hollywood getup and my mom walks in!"

Brandy's friends shouted and groaned at the story. It was their weekly playdate and this time they'd met at Meg's house. Meg loved to try out new gourmet recipes and make fancy cocktails, so about half the time they met at her place because she was dying to try something new out on them.

"Okay, so how did you go from "I'm not dating anyone" to having a nooner at your house with this man?" Angelina demanded.

"We're *not* dating." She might have sounded a tad too defensive, like she was trying to convince herself. Even as she climbed up on that block to stand, it crumbled beneath her feet. Were they dating?

He'd called her Wednesday night to apologize for overstepping with the car. She had apologized, too, because he sounded so sincere. She did appreciate the thought, but it was too much. Then they'd spent the next half hour chatting.

Yes, chatting.

Well, sex-only friends can chat, can't they?

She'd told him about the near scene-wrecker of her mom showing up. They'd laughed together about it. With another guy, she'd be embarrassed. With Justin, she probably would've felt ashamed. He wouldn't want anything socially unacceptable to be revealed. But with Rick, she just felt comfortable to be who she was. It was surprising—shocking, really.

"I don't know, ladies." She stirred her drink, staring at the frozen cantaloupe-mint daiquiri as if the answer to her relationship dilemma might be there. "This may be a huge mistake. He's a player. He's dangerous."

"But you're just playing, right? So no harm done," Angeline said. Her eyes narrowed. "Or are you afraid you're falling for him?"

Gulp.

Was she?

She thought about all the thoughtful things he'd done for her—the headset, entertaining Claire at the hospital, the pizza and movie. The power steering, even though it had pissed her off. It's hard not to fall for a guy that perfect.

She sighed. "I'm not falling for him yet, but I'm afraid I will soon. I thought he'd be full of himself or superficial. Hell, maybe I even thought he'd be a dumb jock, but he isn't any of those things. He is really amazing. The way he's taken it upon himself to help this kid rehab at my gym. Guess what he told me? This can't leave this room, okay?"

The ladies all nodded their eager agreement.

"He said the reason he coaches high school ball instead of college is because his own high school coach made such a difference in his life. He wants to be that guy for other kids. Can you believe this man?"

"Heart of gold," Angelina agreed.

"That's so sweet," Meg said.

"I should write an article about him with that angle—what an amazing guy he is. Am I allowed to say he's playing Santa for the Fostering Christmas event?" Angelina's eyes lit up with the excitement of a good lead.

"Yes, that's been sent out in press releases already. We are hoping his name will help get publicity out there for more donations for the shelter. Just as long as you don't mention anything about our personal relationship, okay?"

"I won't." She tapped her lips, probably already writing the story in her mind.

Juliet rolled her eyes.

Meg slid a tray of hors d'oeuvres on the table.

Brandy reached for a little cracker smeared with goat cheese and topped with a cucumber slice and popped it in her mouth. "Mm, these are heavenly. I want you to cater the opening parties for my new locations."

"Actually... I've been thinking about the event coordinator thing."

"What event coordinator thing?" Juliet looked interested.

"Brandy said she might hire me to handle the parties and grand openings for the new stores."

"Wow... that's a perfect fit," Angelina admitted.

"Well, I know," Meg drawled. "Parties I definitely understand how to do. I mean, I have experience with all aspects of it, from the invitations to the food to the entertainment and decoration." Her conviction had grown, ending with a lift of her chin as if daring one of them to say she didn't.

"Atta girl," Brandy cried. "You'd be perfect at this. When can you start?"

"How about today?"

Angelina lifted her glass. "This calls for a toast! To new ventures."

"To new ventures." They all lifted their glasses and clinked.

* * *

Rick showed up to Phenomenal Physiques already showered. He may be wearing his workout clothes, but he definitely wasn't there to work out.

Yeah, he only had one thing on his mind. Make that one phenomenally physiqued blonde.

Brandy appeared to be waiting for him. She sat behind the desk, an unbuttoned linen blouse pulled on over her yoga top. She also looked fresh and clean. "Good evening Coach Morehouse," she purred when he came in and leaned his forearms on her counter.

"Good evening Ms. Love." He took a quick, surveying glance of the main workout room. Just two people.

"Are you here to work out?" she asked innocently.

"Yes. But I was wondering if you offer anything like... I don't know... a couples workout?"

She flashed a wicked grin. "I've considered trying out a couples yoga class," she drawled, her honeyed voice dripping with naughty innuendo. "It would involve quite a bit of... stretching. But there might be some high impact elements as well. One partner would stretch while the other..." she hit the heel of one hand against the opposite palm, "*impacted.*"

"Mmm." He held her blue eyes. "That sounds like exactly the kind of class I'm looking for. Is it going on tonight?"

She made a show of looking over her shoulder at the white board with the schedule for the day. "It's not on the schedule, but I'm willing to entertain a private. It might cost you a little extra, though."

"Oh yeah? What currencies do you accept?"

She lowered her voice, even though no one was around to hear them. "Orgasms. Cunnilungus. Foot massage. Any of the above, really. I'm pretty open to negotiation when it comes to you. You are a V.I.P. here at Phenomenal Physiques."

"Am I? Well, I'm honored."

She waved a hand toward the display of supplements. "Normally I upsell personal training sessions with supplements, but from what I've observed, you don't have a problem with stamina, do you?"

He smiled. "Flattery will get you everywhere, Ms. Love."

Two women walked past, waving goodbye to Brandy as they left.

"I'll just go put my bag down and check the status of the men's locker room."

Her gaze flicked to the weight room. The two people who had been working out were now gone. "I'll turn some lights off and do a walk-through to see how many are left. Meet me in the massage room. We'll start by warming your muscles up with a little rub-down in there, how's that sound?"

He made an approving sound deep in his throat—somewhere between a growl and a purr. "Sounds good." Like a security guard, he checked every room as he walked down the hall, flicking off lights. One guy was still in the men's locker room, but he stuffed his gym shoes in his bag and left, giving Rick a curious glance as he passed by.

Rick was used to looks, being semi-famous, at least in Houston, so he wasn't sure if it was just that the guy recognized him, or if he wondered why he was showing up at closing time.

He was surprised by the urge to assert his interest in Brandy to the gym customers and the world at large. *Yep, I'm here for the blonde. Hands off her.*

But that was crazy, because A) They didn't have a relationship and B) Even if they did, she wasn't keen on her personal business becoming public. Oh yeah, and C) She still had kids. And dammit, he really didn't know what to do about that show-stopping fact.

* * *

Brandy bade farewell to the last three customers and locked the front door. Alone with Rick at last. She'd been looking forward to this like a lifeline. Especially with the stress of Sam's broken arm and dealing with Justin over football. Actually she hadn't dealt with

Justin, so that was hanging over her head, gnawing in her stomach and keeping her up late at night. Even as she composed nasty diatribes in her head, she knew that wouldn't be the way to approach it. Justin would dig in for a fight, and he'd be more than willing to take her to court over it. She couldn't afford a battle like that—not in money or time. No, she'd have to appeal to Justin's better self, and to do that... well, she needed to relax and get her emotions and stress in check. *To do that she needed smoking hot sex with a sexy football coach.*

So hallelujah for the Saturday night hookup!

She pushed open the door to the massage room and found Rick, leaning against the table, his arms folded across his sexy chest. For a moment, her heart did a little flip flop. He looked so amazing, the open, friendly grin, the wisdom and kindness in those moss-green eyes, the easy-going, yet powerful stance. He took her breath away. "You found it."

"So did you."

He made a show of looking around the room. "So is this where we... test our flexibility?"

"And impact." She waggled her eyebrows.

He chuckled. "I'll show you the kinds of things I may need help with." He reached for her waist and pulled her toward the massage table, spinning her around until she faced it. "See, I've fantasizing about doing something like *this*." He pushed her torso down onto the massage table and hooked his thumbs under the waistband of her yoga pants.

She bit her lip as he dragged them slowly down. She wore them sans panties, so the air hit her bare flesh. The quiver in her thighs had nothing to do with cold, though. Her breath quickened. The pants came all the way off.

Slap.

She gasped at the shock of sensation and sound. Rick had smacked her ass and the crack echoed in the small room.

He immediately rubbed the place he'd slapped, turning the sting into something warm and wonderful. Abruptly, he lifted his hand and brought it down again in exactly the same spot.

"Ow." This time she complained, but his large hand was already rubbing, already soothing. Her clit throbbed, pussy ached for him to touch it, but he just circled the globes of her ass, teasing her, turning her into a trembling mass of desire.

One of his hands reached up to grip her swollen breast.

She moaned.

He pressed his clothed cock against her ass and used both hands to give the twins some attention, cupping and kneading them as he nibbled her neck. With a quick tug, he pulled her yoga top down, causing her breasts to spring free, the stretchy fabric underneath boosting them up into his hands. He pinched both nipples between his fingers and squeezed.

She jerked—the sensation just crossing the line into pain, but he immediately released them and kissed her neck. She dropped her head back against his muscular chest. Her nipples zinged and throbbed, turning her entire body molten. Heat pooled between her legs and a drip of arousal leaked out.

She grasped one of his large hands and dragged it down between her legs.

127

He clapped the other hand down on her ass. "Ah ah. I'm leading tonight."

A wanton sound escaped her lips. She loved this—the way they'd taken turns at control. Loved that he not only demanded her surrender but deserved it, as he'd given her the same trust and satisfaction.

She gritted her teeth, forcing herself to remain passive and let him go at his own pace, even though her entire body screamed for release.

He delivered another spank and rubbed away the sting. He'd had practice at this, she could tell. He walked the line perfectly between pleasure and pain, teasing her with the sensations until they blended into one overwhelming, overriding need.

At last, *at last,* he slid two fingers between her legs.

Her knees nearly buckled from the shock of sensation against her sensitive clit. One leg trembled. A purring noise came from her throat. Or was it a growl? She wanted him inside her so badly, but he continued to tease, lightly brushing his fingers through her wetness, circling her clit, then spanking her ass again.

"Rick..." she moaned, not even sure what she was trying to say or ask.

"Yes, baby?" His fingers penetrated her, delving deep into her slick channel.

She squeezed them with her muscles, desperate for completion.

"What are you doing?" Her voice sounded thick.

He chuckled, a deep rumbling in his chest that seemed to reverberate straight into her pussy. "I am torturing you. Is it working?" He pushed her long hair over to one side and bit her shoulder.

"Oh God," she mumbled. "You need to get on with it. I'm dying here."

"If I didn't have you melting for it, I wouldn't be doing my job, would I?" he rumbled.

"I thought—" she gasped as he pumped his fingers inside her

"Yes?"

"I thought *I* was teaching this class... oh *God*. Please? More?"

"Were you? I guess I got bossy. You want my cock, beautiful?"

"Hell, yeah," she grunted, gripping the opposite edge of the table so tight her knuckles went white.

A foil wrapper crackled, then Rick rubbed the head of his cock against her entrance.

She pushed eagerly back at it.

It was his turn to groan as he slid inside. "*So* good."

She tightened her muscles around his cock.

"Mmm. Do that again. Is this part of your personal training?"

She rolled her forehead around on the massage table. "For special clients," she gasped.

He shoved in hard and immediately pulled almost all the way out.

"Ahhhh-ah." She whimpered at the near loss of him. She needed more. Faster. Harder. "Show me what you've got, big man."

He laughed and gripped her hips. "You think you're ready for what I've got?"

"I'm so ready...*oh*!"

He slammed in hard again, repeating the trick of nearly pulling out.

"I can't believe you're such a tease."

He began to thrust at a more steady rhythm.

"I'm—going—to—make you—pay—for this," she threatened between each delicious instroke.

He pulled all the way out. "Oh yeah?"

"No, no, no, no, no. Just kidding. Please don't stop," she panted.

He laughed again, slapped her ass and slid into her.

"Mmm."

"Is that what you wanted, beautiful?"

"Yes, please." She might have been purring again.

He clapped one large hand over her shoulder to hold her in place as he drilled into her.

Her back bowed, she arched up to meet his thrusts, which forced her breath out of her.

Her clit tingled. "Please, now."

"You want to come?"

"Yeah. Yes, please. Come *on*."

He slammed into her, taking her roughly, harder than she'd ever had it. Her thighs bumped against the table so hard she feared she'd have bruises, but she didn't care. She needed him, craved the punishing force behind each stroke.

At last, when she was just on the verge of cresting without him, he buried himself deep inside her with a shout.

Her muscles spasmed around his thick cock, squeezing him for everything she was worth, the contractions going on and on until they left her rung out like a towel. She let out a long, deliberate exhale and collapsed on the table, boneless. Unable to move.

Rick still shuddered behind her, his muscled thighs flexing and jerking with his cock. When he finished, he bent over her, wrapping one arm around her waist and kissing her neck. "Are you okay?" he murmured.

"Yes," she breathed. "I'm wonderful."

"You certainly are."

He eased out and moved away from her, disposing of the condom. "Who takes out this trash?"

"Hmm?" It took her brain a moment to process the question. She heard the rustle of a plastic bag. "I'm just going to tie this bag up. We don't need anyone finding the evidence of our private lesson."

She eased off the massage table, smiling.

Rick took care of her. He took care of things.

"Where are you going?" He scooped her into his arms.

She whooped in surprise, throwing her arms around his neck. He lifted her as if she weighed nothing, smiling down at her. He was the only man who had ever made her feel petite in comparison to him. She loved it.

He carried her out of the room and her head knocked the Christmas lights strung around the door. She shrieked and giggled. "Where are you taking me?"

"Back to the place we started these games." He grinned. "The men's showers."

* * *

Rick eased Brandy to her feet under a spray of warm water.

She kept her arms looped around his neck,

beaming up at him with that breathtaking smile. He pushed the soap dispenser and rubbed his hands together before smoothing them over her body. He wanted to take it slow this time. To explore every perfect inch of her body. He stroked down her nape and across the backs of her lean, muscular shoulders.

Running his hands down her arms, he squeezed her biceps. "I'll bet some men are intimidated by these guns."

She gave a husky laugh. "Not you."

"No, not me," he murmured, gliding his palms up her sides, from her hips to her breasts, then down the front of her six-pack abs. "You're perfect."

She tried to reach for a handful of her own soap, but he pinned her wrist to the tile wall and traced a finger down the inside of her arm. "My turn, remember?"

"Still?" She gave him pouty lips that stiffened his cock.

With a fresh lather of soap on his palms, he filled his hands with her breasts, stroking light circles around them.

She tipped her face up for a kiss.

He obliged, claiming her mouth with the authority of a man who knows what he wants.

Yes, it was true. He wanted Brandy Love. All of her—not just naked time in the shower. He wanted Sam and Claire. He wanted to meet her friends and her parents. He wanted to be her man. He felt almost light-headed.

He was in too deep. Way too deep.

He didn't know how he would back out now.

Chapter Ten

Brandy's phone rang on the way to her parents' house. A cold, steady drizzle of rain hit the windshield, and the sky was a dull winter grey. Hitting the "answer" button for hands free talking, she said, "Hey you," to Angelina.

"Hi, have you picked up today's *Houston Magazine*?" Angelina asked.

"Not yet, why? Did you write the story about Rick?"

"I sure did. I found some great photos of him in the archives. Solo photos—not the charity event ones with the latest tramp hanging on his arm."

She tried to ignore the rush of jealousy that statement caused. Of course Rick always had a pretty girl on his arm. She'd considered him a bit of a man-whore. But reconciling that with the guy she knew—the coach with a heart of gold—and more, the thoughtful man who had arranged to get her car fixed and entertained her kid in a hospital waiting room... Well, she wanted to think she meant more to him than those pretty girls. But that was foolish. That wasn't what they were doing.

"That sounds great. I can't wait to see it."

"Yeah, my editor liked it so much, they put him on the cover!"

"Way to go! That's exciting." She wasn't mustering enough enthusiasm, still stuck on the tramps from the old archive photos. Or stuck on Rick. And where they were going with this relationship. She was on the verge of getting hurt because she was falling for this guy—ass over tea kettle. And even if she didn't have her own hang-ups about being in a relationship—which she still did, he didn't date single moms.

The pain in her chest made her catch her breath.

"Well, tell me what you think when you see it. And tell me what he says. I'm sure he'll be modest, but I hope he likes it."

"I will definitely fill you in. I'll call you as soon as I read it."

"Okay, have a good night."

She thanked her and disconnected the phone.

Crap. Heartache was not supposed to be on her docket right now. That was the whole point of not dating. Well, that and not having time, although it seemed she'd already dismissed that. She and Rick had somehow found time already, hadn't they?

She pulled into her parents' driveway and climbed out, grabbing the bag of food from Boston Market she'd picked up for them. She tried to drop food off for them at least twice a week, because her mom didn't have time to cook with all the care she gave her dad.

Her mom met her at the door. "He had a bad day," she said in an undertone, holding the screen door open. "Headache. And his arthritis is acting up with this rain. He's been groaning a lot and he didn't want to move from the chair."

She kissed her mom and stepped in, shaking off her soft brown leather jacket. Not the best thing to wear on a rainy day.

She brought the food to the kitchen and greeted her dad in the living room. "Hi Daddy."

He looked like he'd been nodding off in his chair. His eyebrows raised with surprise. "Hello." He took time enunciating the word. Weariness showed in the bags under his eyes and the deepened lines on his face.

Her heart twisted. She hated watching him decline like this. Her mom came in and perched on the arm of his chair, holding his hand.

He smiled and looked up at his wife. For a man who couldn't say much, he expressed himself perfectly. Brandy saw so much love there, pouring out of him. Yes, her parents loved each other dearly. She'd been looking at it as a sort of weakness, but how could she miss how incredibly sweet their partnership was?

Once more, the pang tightened her chest.

She wanted what they had. She did want a life partner, a spouse. Someone who would gaze at her with all the love in his eyes. As if she was the sun itself.

Her eyes smarted with tears. Would she ever have this? With someone?

But no, not "someone." Rick.

And she already knew the answer.

It was no.

* * *

Phil called at 7:00 a.m. Rick was just back from his run and heading for the shower. He shouldn't have picked it up. Nothing good comes of answering the phone at 7:00 a.m. He should have known that.

"Hey Phil."

"Did you see the *Chronicle*?"

He groaned. "What is it this time?"

"The King of Douchebaggery. Stan Brown turned you into some... some... I can't even say." Phil was stuttering. This wasn't good.

"Ugh. You shouldn't read that crap. Don't even tell me."

"No, really. You have to go and read it. It's bad. It's like he's somehow made the rehab you're doing with Donnie into something illegal. It's like he's almost insinuating sexual abuse or something. I'm serious—it's bad. Something needs to be done about this guy."

"I'm not reading it." The last thing he needed was to get sucked into drama with the press. He wouldn't be able to change whatever it was Stan Brown had written in his column. If the a columnist hated him and wanted to make him look bad, there wasn't much he could do about it, and getting himself all wound up wouldn't help.

"No really. This one you need to read. It requires a rebuttal or something."

"I'll see you at the school." It was time to end this conversation.

"I mean it, Rick. Go get the paper."

He hung up on Phil and shook his head, dropping the phone and heading into the shower. Great. A maelstrom of press. Just what he needed right now. First the spread in *Houston Magazine*, making him out to be a hero and now this. Of course the douchebag Stan would have to react to the positive press he'd received in *Houston Magazine* and turn it into something sordid. Right before their playoff game with his kid's team. What an ass.

Rick hadn't liked the *Houston Magazine* article. It wasn't bad—it was meant to be good. It was all about how great a guy he was and his special training work with Donnie. But he didn't need his ego stroked that way and what bothered him was that the source had obviously been Brandy. Had it just been to get a mention about her gym?

Had she been using him this whole time? She *was* an ambitious business woman.

But she should have asked him first before she did a reveal all. This felt like a betrayal and it left a sour taste in his mouth.

Maybe this was a sign that it was time to pull back.

He'd already bent his rule about not getting too involved. Hell, before this went down, he'd been fantasizing about what it'd be like to be her man. Forever.

But now it looked like she'd been using him. Or at best, had been opportunistic with his fame and reputation. He didn't like it.

When she'd texted the night before he'd let it go unanswered.

Tonight, perhaps, when he went over there with Donnie.

He finished his daily workout, lifting hand weights and doing his squats and burpees.

His phone rang again. It wasn't even 8:00 yet. He glanced at the number and his throat closed.

His dad. What in the hell did he want?

He stared at the ringing phone. His brain had

stuttered to a halt, the old childhood resentment battling with his no-drama policy. Five rings and the thing went to voicemail. Fine. Good. He had nothing to say to the man, anyway.

Shaking his head, he headed for his shower.

Damn, this day wasn't shaping up to be a good one.

* * *

Brandy called an emergency lunch playdate. If ever she'd needed her friends, it was now. Her brain was so muddled, she didn't know what to think about anything. Rick hadn't texted or called her back—it had been over 24 hours. That was weird. She figured he was mad about Angelina's article yesterday, and with today's horrible column in the *Chronicle*, she feared he'd hate her forever. He certainly had to blame her. The press never would have had the scoop on the work he was doing with Donnie if she hadn't blabbed it to Angelina. And she'd known Angelina intended to write an article and hadn't even tried to stop her. Her only concern had been that their relationship not be mentioned. She really should have asked Rick for permission first.

She got a booth for four at Americas and sat down, swirling a plantain chip in the olive oil and lemon mixture while she waited.

She rested her cheek on one hand and drummed her fingernails on the table. Where should she go with all this?

Angelina found her and scooted in first. Her eyes were wide and her forehead was crinkled in concern.

She dropped the open sports section of the *Houston Chronicle* on the table. "Honey, I'm so sorry about that stupid column. That was so far off-base. I mean, seriously, someone needs to dump that man in a swamp with alligators."

"Agreed," she said.

"What does Rick say?"

Meg showed up and slid in beside her. "Yeah, what does Rick say?"

"Wait, wait, wait," Juliet said, scooting into her side. "I want the whole scoop."

"There's nothing to tell," she moaned. "He hasn't returned my texts or calls. He must be seriously pissed off. I never should have given out information about him." It took great effort, but she didn't glare at Angelina. It was her own fault and she had to own her responsibility for the consequences.

"Well, the paper made it sound like he's doing something illegal, and if not illegal, certainly unethical. It said he's secretly giving certain boys special help off school grounds to make the school more competitive. And it implies that he might be affecting the boy's chances of getting into college."

"That's total bullshit!" Her face had grown hot, as if she was the accused. "I don't believe there's any school policy against working off-site. But even if there is what's the big deal? What, he's sexually abusing this kid or something? It almost seemed like he was implying that! Jesus, what a mess." Her stomach had twisted into a tight knot. She felt so horribly responsible.

"That Stan Brown is a real asshole. He should be in politics, because he's the type who could spin every single positive trait in his opponent into a negative one," Juliet said.

"Something should be done about him," she muttered.

The waitress came, but none of them had even looked at the menu. They snatched them up and chose quickly, since none of them had time to make it a two-hour lunch.

"What should I do?" she moaned. She seriously needed her friends to just tell her, because all her gears had locked up.

"Are you asking what can you do about the article? Or what can you do about your relationship with Rick?" Juliet asked.

She drew in a shaky breath. "Well, I care about what happens to Rick. And I feel responsible for this fiasco." She waved her hand at the newspaper lying on the table. "But really what I'm upset about is..." She drew a deep breath. "Ladies, *I really like this guy.*"

There. She'd admitted it.

And because they were awesome friends, none of them made her eat crow about not dating or not having a relationship.

"Oh, honey." Meg covered her hand with her own. "He's a great guy. I can see why you don't want something like this to end things."

End things?

She felt like she'd been hit by a brick in the chest.

Meg thought this would end things.

Tears stung her eyes. "I don't even know if we're even at a stage in which there are things to be ended," she croaked. "But yeah, I definitely don't want it to be over like this."

Meg squeezed her hand and five pairs of sympathetic eyes surrounded her.

Fortunately the waitress brought their iced teas at that moment, and she pulled herself together.

"So what can Brandy do?" Meg asked the group. "If you were Rick, what would you want her to do?"

"He might need a little time. I mean, you should definitely apologize immediately, but don't freak out if he's not ready to accept it," Meg suggested. "Have you tried to apologize yet?"

"Yeah." She sighed. "I tried calling this morning and when he didn't answer, I texted him. He still hasn't answered."

"Okay, don't panic. Remember that *Men are from Mars* book? They need to go into their man cave to sit alone with their problems. They don't hash them out with friends, like we do," Juliet said.

A wave of gratitude for her friends swept over her. She reached her empty hand out to grab Juliet's hand and squeeze it. "I'm so glad I have friends," she said, her smile wobbling.

"It's going to be all right," Meg soothed. "I'm sure it will be fine."

"Are you sure?" She really just needed them to tell her everything was going to work out. She'd never felt so helpless in her life.

"Yes. It will work out. Don't worry." Three voices assured her.

"And what about the article? Won't it just blow over?"

"I'm not sure. That kid's mom may be calling up the principal and freaking out right now. Or there might be pressure from the board to do something. But I doubt

141

there's any way he'd get fired, unless someone can really prove some terrible wrongdoing." This analysis came from Juliet and Brandy didn't find it comforting. Not in the least. In fact, it sounded worse than ever.

"Oh God…" she covered her mouth with her hand and slumped down in her seat.

"Aren't you buddy-buddy with the district superintendent?" Juliet asked.

She stared at her blankly. "Huh?"

"The superintendent. He was at one of my campaign parties and you seemed to know him."

"Ohhh. That was Justin. Yeah, they're racquetball buddies. But he wouldn't have a clue who I am without Justin. Why?"

"I'm thinking Justin should call him up and give him a little legal advice about the situation. Mainly, that it's no big deal and the district should say *no comment* to the press and ignore the rest."

She stared at Juliet, her brain trying that idea on for size. She shook her head. "Justin wouldn't help. He's been a total prick about football. He doesn't want Sam to play, so he probably relishes Rick's problems right now."

"I doubt that," Juliet chided.

She scowled. It was easy to blame Justin for everything, but Juliet was right, Justin wasn't mean. Although he might be if he knew she and Rick were dating.

"Okay, so I should give Rick some space, but if I can get in contact with the superintendent, I should tell him not to worry."

Her friends laughed, realizing how impossible both of those tasks sounded.

"Someone tell me something funny?"

"I had sex last night," Meg said in a small voice.

Three heads swiveled. "Er... with your husband?"

"Yeah." She blushed. "You guys were right, I just needed something else to do. I've been super busy planning Brandy's Fostering Christmas event and I guess I was cheerful about it. So I was humming in the living room, prepping the stocking bags, and Teddy came up behind me and kissed my neck. He said he was glad to see me so happy. And guess what? Suddenly all our problems didn't seem that big." Her smile looked guilty.

Juliet held her palm up for a high five. "Way to go, sister. Good sex goes a long way to fixing a marriage."

Meg lifted her shoulders. "I don't know," she drawled. "I'm not sayin' things are *fixed*, but they certainly are better." She put her lips around her straw, a new spark of life in her eye.

The tightness in Brandy's solar plexus hadn't left, but she was grateful to Meg for the distraction. And so very happy for her friend.

At least one thing was right in the world.

* * *

Rick slammed his palm down on Houston High's principal, Ted Bristol's desk more forcefully than he meant to. Dave and Phil stood behind him like his wingmen, matching glowers on their faces.

Ted spread his palms, his bald head shining under the florescent glare. "It's out of my hands. It came straight from the superintendent. You're suspended until the board can review the ethics involved in the case."

"What case?" Dave sputtered. "There is no case! A

crack pot wanna-be journalist wrote an inflammatory column, and now suddenly there's a 'case?'"

"Donald Fleming's mother called. She's concerned the allegation may hurt her son's chance for college recruitment."

Phil rolled his eyes. "The whole reason Rick was working with him was to improve his chances. Rick is personally delivering Donnie to his pal at Texas A&M, who will be watching tonight's playoff game."

Ted shifted in his chair, his oversized belly hitting the top of the desk. "Well, that's what I told her. The board just wants to meet to discuss the ethics of this before it goes any further."

"How can it go further? This could be the last game of the season?" Phil pointed out.

Dave jumped back in, "Just because some armchair quarterback—*whose son happens to play for Coral Heights, I must point out*— conjectures the opposite, it's true? Who are you going to trust? A man who's been successfully coaching here for the past ten years or—"

"Yeah, yeah. You are preaching to the choir. I told you, it's out of my hands." Ted made a pushing motion with his hands, like he wanted to shoo them out of his office.

"No, seriously. It's no coincidence this article came out on the day of playoffs against Coral Heights. I guarantee you he was trying to screw up our game for tonight, and you're letting it happen. Do you even *care* if we take State? Because I'm sure the kids in Odessa will be celebrating this disaster, too."

"Did you even defend Rick to the superintendent?" Dave asked.

Rick didn't want to hear any more of this. He turned and pushed past his two defenders and out of the office. "Come on, guys. This is pointless. Save your energy for beating Coral Heights."

"No working off school grounds, either!" Ted called after them from his office.

Dave actually flipped him the bird. Yeah, so high school coaches could be about as mature as the kids that played for them, sometimes. At this moment, Rick didn't give a flying fuck.

"So what is our plan?" Phil asked.

The bell had just rung between classes so they walked out to the stares of almost every kid in the crowded corridor. The kids may not read the paper themselves, but their parents had and he had to imagine rumors were running like wildfire about him right now.

Rick stalked out to the parking lot. "Just stick to the playbook, heavy on the pass plays."

Damn, it killed him to be away from the most important game of the season.

"Yeah, I'll handle it. We'll be okay. Will you come and watch? From the stands, I mean?"

"Nothing would keep me away," he said through gritted teeth. The school was public property, so unless the superintendent planned on getting a restraining order, he'd be there.

Dave clapped him on the shoulder. "We'll get this worked out. Hopefully before the game on Friday. This whole town loves you, with the exception of the King of Douchebaggery. I'll bet it's resolved by the end of the day."

He shook his head, anger burning him up. He

didn't usually let things get to him, but this situation screamed bullshit. He climbed in his Escalade and glanced at his phone. A voicemail from his mom and Brandy's unanswered texts.

He shot of a single line, *Superintendent suspended me pending investigation.*

It was wrong of him, but he hoped she felt bad. Of course she hadn't meant to hurt him. But maybe this was a sign. He'd been getting in way too deep with her. This gave him a reason to back off.

Yes, what he needed was to back way the hell off. Even when this shitstorm finally settled—if it finally settled, he wouldn't go back to the gym. It was easier this way. Cleaner.

Why did it feel like he'd been stabbed in the middle of his chest?

* * *

Brandy had to sit down when she read Rick's text. No, more like she would've fallen down, but fortunately there was a chair behind her. She slumped into it staring at the words, her brain stuttering and stalling. It couldn't be. Why would they do something like that to Rick?

And oh, God, it was her fault! Well, it was mostly that jackass Stan Brown's fault, but still—she was the one who gabbed about Rick's extracurricular generosity. This was terrible.

"Are you all right?" Jennie's concerned voice broke through her fog.

"Huh? Oh, um... not really. Listen, something's come up. I need to go see someone. I'll be back in time to teach my class, though, okay?"

"Okay, sure. Anything I can do to help?"

"No thanks. I—only I can do this."

She got in her SUV and pulled out of the parking lot.

This was terrible—for Rick, for the kids he coached, for Sam. And yes, for herself. Because despite what she'd been insisting all along about not wanting a relationship, she'd been lying. She wanted Rick in her life on a permanent basis. And that may be impossible. He may never even speak to her again after all this, but she owed it to him to fix this problem. And she owed it to herself to at least clear the obstacles she'd laid in their path.

If Rick still wanted nothing to do with her, that would be his decision.

She drove downtown, weaving through the heavy noontime Houston traffic. After pulling into a parking garage, she grabbed her purse and headed for the elevator to the Anderson, Jacobs and Henze Law Firm.

She needed Justin's help.

With her purse clasped before her, she stood in the elevator, drawing deep breaths. There was only one way to recruit Justin. It wasn't through arguing her case, because she had never, in the history of their relationship, won that way. No, she'd have to do something she should have done a long time ago—forgive him.

She exited the elevator and opened the glass doors to the reception area. The receptionist's brows shot up.

"Hi Carol, how are you?"

Carol was still getting over her shock at seeing her here, post-divorce. "H-hello, Brandy."

"Is Justin available? He's not expecting me."

Curiosity shone in Carol's eyes, but she picked the phone up and hit a button. With her head lowered, she said in a low tone, "Yes, Brandy is here to see you." Justin must have been as incredulous as Carol because she said, "Brandy Anderson—or, um... yes, your ex-wife."

The door down the hall opened and Justin's tall, lanky frame leaned out. His brows were down as he surveyed her.

She forced a smile and offered a small wave.

He beckoned her back with a short, authoritative curl of his fingers.

Screwing up her courage, she stood and walked back to his office.

Do not be defensive. Let it go. You loved him once.

"What's going on?" he demanded, still holding the door open for her.

She walked into the office and sat down on the client side of his huge, mahogany desk. "Did you see the paper today?"

Damn, that wasn't how she meant to lead this conversation.

He walked around behind the desk and sat down. "Yeah, the coach thing? I knew it wasn't a good idea for Sam to go—"

She gave a sharp shake of her head and held up her hand. "That's what I wanted to talk to you about. Well, that and a bunch of things, really."

He pursed his lips. "I don't understand." He was a good-looking man. She'd lost sight of that in their last, ugly year, but looking at him now, she remembered why she'd found him attractive. He'd certainly contributed good genes to making their beautiful children. For that, she would forever be grateful.

She blinked, not sure how to start. She wasn't even sure what she wanted to say. All she knew is the outcome she needed from this conversation.

"First of all, I just wanted to... apologize."

Okay, she surprised herself. She hadn't been planning on that.

Justin's face remained impassive.

"I... I know I was the one who changed in our relationship. You were a good husband and a good father and we had a good thing going."

A flicker of some emotion crossed Justin's face. "I don't know where you're going with this." That was his defensive, lawyerly side. The one she didn't want to be talking to.

"It's just something I've been thinking about. I guess I blamed you for not wanting things to change. I felt like you were holding me back. But it's not your fault that I became a different person than the one you married."

Justin blinked at her.

"So, I'm sorry. I mean, I'm not sorry for moving on and pursuing my dreams, but I am sorry that it hurt you. You didn't deserve that."

Something definitely moved behind Justin's mask. He stood up and paced to the window, staring down. "You want me to greenlight Sam's football career."

Damn, he made her sound so manipulative when he put it that way.

"I don't want our past challenges to affect

decisions about the kids. It's not fair to them."

Justin was silent for a long time. "Sam really wants this?"

She heard the concession in his voice. "He does. I didn't push him into this, although I obviously support his interest."

Justin turned back and shoved his hands in his pockets. "Okay."

Her heart rolled over. She tried not to look too thrilled. "Thanks, Justin. It means a lot to Sam."

"But we don't even know if Morehouse will be at the high school next year."

Here goes.

"That's the other thing I wanted to talk to you about. You see, this whole thing is my fault. I told Angelina about him working with the student at my gym, and she wrote an article in *Houston* Magazine. Then that stupid columnist twisted it around into something bizarre and wrong."

Justin nodded. "Yeah, it sounds like nothing more than a tempest in a teapot if you ask me."

"I heard Dr. Perricone, the superintendent, suspended him while they look into it."

Justin lifted his shoulders as if to say, "So?"

"I'm responsible for all this getting started in the first place. I feel terrible that his career and reputation may be on the line, not to mention concerned for Sam's sake. I was thinking maybe Dr. Perricone just needs a little legal advice. You know, you could tell him this is nothing."

Justin chuckled. "Oh, now I see where you're going with this. Well, I don't know if I can do anything—"

"Will you try?" She gave him puppy eyes. It was like old times, now, the rancor and defensiveness between them gone, at least for the moment.

"Sure, I'll try."

She jumped to her feet. "Really?"

"I don't know if it will do any good."

She threw her arms around him and gave him a hug. He froze and patted her awkwardly on the shoulder and she stepped back. "Sorry... thanks. I appreciate it. Will you let me know how it goes?"

He nodded. "Yeah, I'll let you know."

"Thanks. Again. Really." She grabbed her bag and headed to the door. She put her hand on the handle and paused. "I really hope... well, I just wish you the best."

He nodded, hands stuffed in his pockets again. "Yeah, you too. Good luck with the new gyms you're opening."

She smiled, a genuine, grateful smile. "You too. I mean—good luck with your practice and everything." What she wanted to say was that she hoped he'd find another woman. Someone who made him happy this time. But things were still too raw to say that. Or it wasn't her place, anyway.

"Bye."

"I'll see you later."

She slipped out and smiled at Carol as she walked out. Well, she'd played her only ace. Hopefully it would be enough.

* * *

Rick's day only got worse. When he stepped off the elevator to his condo, he found a man standing at his door.

No. Fucking. Way.

"What are you doing here?"

The old man winced. He had bags under his eyes and paunchy cheeks. His teeth were stained yellow and his skin tone had a grey tinge to it. "I tried to call but you didn't pick up."

Rick didn't move any closer to his door and his dad—yeah, his dear old absent *dad*—just stood there. Once a large man like Rick, his father now looked diminished—shoulders slumped, body thinned out.

"What are you doing here?" he repeated.

His dad had been totally absent for his childhood. He'd moved to Florida when Rick was three and rarely attempted to contact him or his mother. Of course, he wouldn't want them to know his exact whereabouts, because then his mother would've been able to file for child support. No, his dad had dodged all financial responsibility for Rick. He'd just sent occasional lame presents that showed he had no idea what age his son was or what his interests were.

Then Rick had been picked by the Houston, Texans, and suddenly his dad had shown up, eager to claim him. Well, eager to claim some share of the riches he was sure Rick had.

His father tucked his hands in the pockets of a worn leather bomber jacket—the kind that had been popular about 30 years ago. "I came to see you."

Well, that was obvious.

"What for?"

"Can I come in?"

He didn't bother to hide his annoyance, but he pulled out his keys and unlocked the door, holding it open. "Listen, It hasn't been a good day. I really don't

152

have the time or the patience for whatever grand reunion you have planned."

"I saw the article in the paper. That guy's a real prick. Anyone who read it must know he's full of crap."

Rick shrugged.

His dad pulled out one of the barstools at the breakfast bar. "Can I sit?"

Rick ignored him, walking to the refrigerator and pulling it open. He stared unseeingly at the food inside. He'd suddenly lost his appetite.

"I know you don't want me in your life. I missed out on the time when you did, and now it's too late."

"Yep."

"I can't change what I've done. I was a shitty father, I know that."

"You said it." He swung the refrigerator door shut. Definitely not hungry.

"Rick... I'm dying. I'm on hospice. Pancreatic cancer."

Jesus fucking Christ. It felt like he'd been punched in the gut. Was the man really throwing this at him right now? He'd like a do-over on the whole damn day. Was he supposed to care? The fuck of it was that he did. Sort of. He may not care about this particular man, who was a stranger to him, but he did care that his father was going to be dead. Soon.

"How long?" he managed to say.

"Don't know. A couple months, maybe. I'm moving here."

"Here here?" He pointed at his floor. "Like, to my place?"

"No, no, no. I know you don't want me. No, I got

Medicare. The social worker in Florida found me a place here."

Rick couldn't breathe, the image of his father dying in some shit-shack disgusting him. "Well, where is it? Will you be alone or is there someone to take care of you? How's this supposed to work?"

"I'll be alone for a while, but a nurse will come to the house once a week and if she decides I need more help, they'll put me in one of them full time homes."

Rick's nose burned. Pressure built behind his cheekbones, so he felt like he face would burst. "Okay." He nodded. He really couldn't think what else to say.

His father was dying.

"I'm sorry I wasn't ever there for you. I just... after your mom threw me out... I was drinking back then and I didn't know my head from my ass. I thought about you all the time, but I figured you were better off without me."

Rick worked to swallow. He wanted to say "bullshit," except he realized it was probably true. If his dad was drunk all the time, he wouldn't have had money to send for child support. And yeah, Rick probably was better off without him. "Mom threw you out?"

He'd never heard that part before.

"Yeah, I can't remember what for. She got sick of me drinking, I guess. And then, after I lost you and her... well, there was no point in pulling my life together. At least that's how it seemed at the time."

Rick shoved his fingers through his hair. "Look... I don't even know what to say. I've got a playoff game tonight that I've been suspended from coaching and a recruiter from Texas A&M to entertain. I've got kids depending on me who I'm going to let down if I don't work some shit out."

His father stood up, holding out his hands. "Yeah, I get it. I won't stay."

A stab of guilt sliced his solar plexus. But why should he feel guilty? His father certainly hadn't. Maybe this cancer thing was just a ploy.

But no, the old man looked horrible. Rick pitied him, he really did, but he couldn't bring himself to care about him. He was no more than a stranger. He may have lent his genes, but that was it.

"I... I'll talk to you later." It was a lame thing to say, and the sadness in his father's eyes said he didn't believe it. Rick wasn't sure whether he meant it or not.

"Yeah. Okay, son. I'll let myself out. Bye, now."

He stared blankly at the kitchen table, listening to the door click shut behind his father.

He really didn't have it in him to deal with this.

* * *

Brandy checked her phone all day for a message from Justin. She knew Houston High's playoffs were that night, so if they didn't get the superintendent to reverse his decision to suspend Rick, the team's chances at State might be affected.

She'd told the kids they would attend the game, but now her stomach twisted every time she thought about it. She couldn't bear the thought of sitting in the bleachers and watching a game being coached by someone else. Because of her.

And... oh God... her chest really hurt thinking about never seeing Rick again.

When she hadn't heard from Justin by the end of the day, she texted him. *Have you talked to Dr. Perricone?*

He texted back, *No, he hasn't called me back. Probably has all of Houston calling him.*

Ugh. She wanted to tell Justin he should keep trying, but she didn't want to press her luck. To her surprise, he texted again, *Are you taking the kids to the game?*

Yes.

If I don't hear, I'll come, too. Perricone will surely be there.

Wow. Was Justin going out of his way to help her? Or, if not her, the situation? Sheesh. She should have tried a dose of forgiveness and olive branch extending a long time ago. It might have saved them both a lot of heartache.

She texted, *Don't call me Shirley.* It was an old, dumb joke, and she probably shouldn't be joking with Justin. They were over, after all. But she figured they both could lighten up a little. Hopefully he wouldn't think she was flirting or trying to get back together.

No, he must know they had a clean break.

She and the kids drove to the stadium and parked a block away on the street because the lot was already full. She explained to them why Rick wasn't coaching tonight and both were furious on his behalf. Her kids really liked Rick.

Kids spilled out of decorated cars, faces splashed in war paint, wearing either orange and black for the Houston High Tigers or green and yellow for Coral Heights.

She wondered where that asshole Stan Brown was. He was lucky he didn't use a photo for his column, or Houston High's fans would probably hunt him down and kill him right now. She'd sure like to give him a piece of her mind. They walked into the stadium, heading toward the orange and black side. The school marching band played an upbeat song— wait, was that "Octopus' Garden" by the Beatles?

"Hey mom, there's my friend, Liam—from the clinic? Can I go and sit with him?"

"Oh—" she tried to hide her disappointment. She still wasn't used to her kids preferring their friends to mom. This teenager stuff was rough. "Sure, honey. Do you have your cell phone?"

Sam patted his pocket. "Yep."

"Okay, keep it on, in case I can't find you."

"Okay, mom—see you later." He dashed off, a wide grin splitting his face.

At least she still had Claire. "Where should we sit, kiddo?" They surveyed the packed bleachers.

Claire pointed way up toward the top, where a few empty places remained and they headed up. "Can I have a snack?"

Damn, she hadn't given Sam any money for food. Well, hopefully he'd find her when he got hungry. "Sure, honey." She dug in her purse for her wallet and handed it to Claire. "Get me a hotdog?"

Claire grabbed the wallet. Only a year ago she would've been too shy to go and order food on her own, but now she seemed to love the freedom. Brandy normally loved it—she used to complain it was "parent abuse" when Claire would make her get up and order something for her if Sam wasn't around to go with her.

This time, though, as Brandy walked up the bleacher steps, she'd never felt more alone.

Was Rick here, somewhere? Had he worked things out with the superintendent? Or was he in the bleachers like her? She scanned the crowd, searching, but it was too packed, even with Rick's big frame, she wouldn't be able to pick him out.

She sighed and found two seats way up high in the bleachers and settled down to watch the pre-game excitement.

She pulled her phone out and checked to see if Rick or Justin had sent any messages. None. She composed a text to Rick. *My ex is friends with Perricone. Trying to get his ear to get you reinstated before game,* she wrote.

No.

She deleted it. That somehow made it sound like she was trying to take credit for saving the day, when she was partly responsible for ruining it. She wanted him to know she was trying, but couldn't think of a way to do it. Well, she'd just have to wait to see what the outcome of Justin's efforts were.

Claire slid in beside her, holding a hot dog and a basket of jalapeno nachos.

"Thanks, hon."

And then she saw him. Rick was seated in the middle front row of the stands. On one side of him sat an overweight bald man. On the other side—Dr. Perricone and Justin. She sucked in her breath. It did something strange to her tummy to see Justin and Rick sitting together. Her past and her future partners... at least, she hoped.

"Mom, is that Daddy down there with Coach Morehouse?"

"Yes." She sounded slightly breathless.

"Are they friends?"

"Um... no, honey, probably not."

"What's Daddy doing down there?"

"He's trying to help Coach Morehouse get back on the field."

"Can he help? Will it work?"

"I don't know, baby. I sure hope so." She set her hotdog down beside her and wiped clammy hands on her jeans.

The band's drum section was beating out a lively rhythm. Anticipation shimmered in the air, pulsing with the music, with her heartbeat.

More than a game hung on the line. Her entire happiness, her future had also tangled up with this game. She wanted Rick back on the field, wanted the team to win, wanted Rick to forgive her.

But even if all those things happened, it didn't mean Rick wanted a relationship.

And that notion depressed the hell out of her.

Chapter Eleven

Rick's fists tightened at his sides. He was supposed to be sitting with his buddy Blake Elway, the scout from Texas A&M, but Blake hadn't shown up yet.

Instead, he was stuck beside his principal and superintendent and Brandy's ex—three of the people he least wanted to be near at this moment. He'd arrived early to stake out a good place and for some reason, Bristol and Perricone decided to flank him. And then Brandy's ex showed up.

Donnie came running into the stands in his full uniform and helmet, his face pinched with worry. Rick surged to his feet. "What are you doing up here, Donnie? You should be in the locker room with the team."

"Coach, I have to talk to you."

He glanced over his shoulder at the principal and superintendent. "Donnie, bring it to Coach Dinsmore. I'm not on duty tonight."

"I know, but I gotta talk to you. To *you*, Coach."

"What is it?" Holes burned in his back from the stares of Dr. Perricone and Ted. "What is this about? You nervous about the scout? Don't even think about him. Just play your best."

160

"No, that's not it—"

"Donnie, what's going on?" Donnie's mother called out from the next bench down.

The announcer came on to welcome them to the game. His voice could barely be heard over the din of the crowd. The doors to the field opened and the Coral Heights players ran out. The Houston High side booed. Normally Houston High fans showed better sportsmanship, but he supposed with Stan Brown's article, everyone's claws were bared.

"Donnie, get your head together and get out there with your team. You got this." He slapped him on the butt. "*Go.*"

Donnie cast him a panicked looked, but it wasn't in him to disobey. He turned and ran back down the stairs to the locker room.

The band picked up as the Houston High players ran out from their side.

He looked back at Ted and Perricone. Fuck it, he was going to move. Without any explanation, he walked down to where Donnie's mom and sister sat. "Mind if I sit here?"

"Of course not!" Everyone on the bench shuffled down, making him a space where there had been none.

"What's wrong with Donnie?" Mrs. Fleming demanded.

He shook his head. "I don't know what that was about. Just nerves, probably." It wasn't like Donnie to have a case of nerves, though. If anything, the kid was too cocky. He wondered if he'd reinjured his knee. Well, Dave and Phil would have to take care of it, if that was the case. Rick wasn't coaching tonight.

Houston High won the coin toss and received the

kick-off. On first down they ran their favorite play-action pass play, 35 dive Omaha post, but Coral Heights seemed to anticipate their moves, intercepting the ball and running with it.

"Get on him," he roared, jumping to his feet. Jesus, he hated being up here in the stands. He didn't want to watch a football game sitting down. He needed to be down on the field, pacing, watching from the sidelines.

Dammit.

"No... no, *no!*" Coral Heights returned it all the way for a touchdown.

What a disaster. This was not a good way to start off the first play of the game.

He gritted his teeth as the extra point split the uprights.

Coral Heights lined up and kicked off. It was a short kick, taken by one of Houston High's blockers. Coral Heights swarmed the ball carrier, causing a fumble which Coral Heights recovered.

"Protect the ball!"

Coral Heights' offense took the field. Houston High responded strongly, sacking their quarterback, causing them to lose ten yards.

"That's it, boys, keep it up." He clapped with the rest of the crowd.

On the field, Dave and Phil stood with their heads huddled together. He'd give anything to be down there with them. This was total bullshit.

Second down, Coral Heights made their pass, but the Houston High defense tackled them at the 40-yard line.

Third down, Coral Heights lost five yards.

On fourth down, Coral Heights lined up to punt but instead faked the kick and threw the ball downfield to a wide open receiver. Touchdown. Again.

Holy hell, this game was not going well.

His phone buzzed. Blake, the scout from Texas A&M, texted, *What's going on with your team this year?*

He blew his breath out with a hiss. He didn't even know how to respond. He'd do damage control after the game with Blake.

Houston High had the ball. Coral Heights had a better offense than defense, so this was their chance to catch up. Once more, the teams lined up. The play was the unbalanced left wildcat 37 reverse.

Incredibly, Coral Heights seemed to anticipate the play again, taking them down before they even got started.

"What?" Donnie's mom yelled beside him. The fans booed.

Something wasn't right here. Coral Heights was a good team—that's how they made it to the playoffs, but even if they'd sent someone to watch every Houston High game, they wouldn't be able to anticipate their plays like this.

He rubbed his face.

The next three plays were equally well-defended and Houston High lost the ball. They were down fourteen to zero and Coral Heights had the ball.

Not good.

Coral Heights scored again. His team had lost their mojo down there. Whether it was because of the drama surrounding his suspension or the uncanny way Coral Heights seemed to anticipate their plays, something was off. Big time.

Twenty-one to zero. Tension in the stands only increased his own. Even from where he sat, he could see the sagging posture of his boys, the desperation on their expressions. They were more than sweating it. They needed guidance.

Fuck. They needed him.

They set up the next play, the WideSwing, 22 Sneak. The Coral Heights defense moved in choreographed response, anticipating each player's move.

"They have our playbook."

He hadn't wanted to say it before, hadn't wanted to believe it was true. But there was no denying it. These kids weren't getting lucky. No, they knew exactly what they were doing.

"What did you say, Coach?" Mrs. Fleming demanded. Her eyes flashed with anger.

He gestured furiously toward the field. "They have our playbook. Somehow, someone got ahold of our playbook and gave it to Coral Heights."

Mrs. Fleming's nostrils flared. "It was that girl." Her daughter leaned forward, eyes wide.

"What girl?"

"Donnie's girlfriend—Tessa. He had her over at the house yesterday. I don't like her. I never have. *And she's from Coral Heights.*"

The image of Donnie's pinched, worried face flashed in front of his eyes.

Oh shit. Had the kid lost his playbook? To a girl? Well, dammit, why hadn't he told Dave or Phil by now? But no, he already knew. Donnie had never bonded with the other coaches. That's why he'd been up here in the stands trying to talk to Rick.

He stabbed his fingers through his hair, wishing to hell he'd given the kid one minute when he'd come.

Once more his team lined up.

Jesus, he hoped Dave and Phil had figured out what was going on and changed something—anything—up. Hell, if they'd let the boys play free-for-all, it would go better than this.

He smacked his forehead with his hand and left it there, rubbing, not wanting to see the total debacle on the field. "Donnie's dating a girl from Coral Heights?" He'd heard her, he just couldn't believe it. Was the kid nuts? Or stupid?

"Mm hmm. I'm telling you, I never liked that girl. Prissy little white girl hanging all over him. Not his type at all. I *knew* she was trouble. She was over last night. *Last night.* Donnie said they were studying together."

"I told them they had to keep the bedroom door open. I was worried about—" her eyes darted to her daughter and she closed her lips, raising her eyebrows. "Looks like I was worried for the wrong reason."

He stood up. He needed to get down there. If Perricone wanted to fire him, he could do it, but he'd be damned if he was going to let this ship sink without stepping in to help.

Coral Heights intercepted another pass. Hell.

He stalked past the principal and superintendent as Coral Heights scored again. *Fuck.* This was a bloodbath.

* * *

As he headed to the locker room, he passed Phil, who looked pale. "Amy's in labor. I'm sorry, Rick, I've held out as long as I could, but the contractions are five minutes apart. If I miss this birth—"

Jesus. What more could go wrong? Not that Phil's baby was wrong, but bad timing, for sure.

"*Go!* Don't worry about the game. I'll take care of it."

"You will? How? Nevermind, text me the news!"

"You text me the news!" he called after Phil's retreating back.

The energy in the locker room crackled with tension. The clang of a fists slamming into metal locker reached him before he made out what the angry voices were saying.

"They have our fucking playbook!" one of the kids yelled.

"Language, Ames," he called out sharply, before he'd even rounded the corner into the locker room. The crowd fell silent, recognizing his voice. Everyone stared.

"You may be angry, but that's no excuse to lose your composure. In fact, if I ever needed you guys to keep it together more, it's right now." He put his hands on his hips and narrowed his eyes, taking the time to make contact with each boy's gaze.

Donnie wouldn't make eye contact. He had his helmet off, and sat slumped on a bench, staring at his hands.

"They have our playbook. So what do we do?"

"How did they get it? Who gave it to them?" someone demanded.

He shook his head. "Right now, that doesn't matter. What matters is beating Coral Heights. They've pulled out the dirtiest tricks this game. Are you going let them get away with this?"

The boys shook their heads.

He raised his voice, "I said, *are you going to let them get away with this?*"

"No, Coach Morehouse!" the boys shouted.

He nailed them each with a hard stare. "Good. The playbook will be their downfall, my friends. Here's what we're going to do."

He reached for Dave's copy of the playbook and opened to the page for what should be the next play of the game. "We change each one just slightly. They'll think they know what's going to happen, and by the time they realize it's not the play they expected, it will be too late. This may only work once or twice. After that, they'll stop trying to anticipate and just play a normal game, so let's make those first couple times count."

He pointed at the next play and held his hand out. Dave scrambled to hand him a dry erase marker. "Here's what we're going to do." He went through the next plays, changing only one thing about each. He kept it simple so the boys could remember without having practiced the plays.

"Everyone understand?"

The boys nodded.

"We're out of time," Dave said, looking at his watch.

"No mercy on them," he said, narrowing his eyes.

"No mercy," a couple kids muttered.

"Say it together."

"No mercy!" the boys shouted and put their helmets back on.

"Get out there and show them what happens to cheaters."

167

Their anger channeled, the boys jogged out, jaws set, eyebrows down.

When Donnie passed him, he caught him by the facemask and pulled him off to the side. The kid paled, face drawn up in dread. Kids get kicked off teams for losing their playbooks, and this team would probably never forgive him if they found out. Donnie's entire football career rested on this game. He'd been out with the knee injury when other scouts had come, so this was his only shot.

He gripped Donnie's helmet in both hands and pulled his face up close. "Did you lose your playbook?"

He kept his voice low, so the others wouldn't hear.

Anguish scrunched up Donnie's face. He blinked rapidly. "Coach..."

"Your girlfriend took it?"

"I'm sorry, Coach," he croaked.

"Me too, Donnie. You fucked up. Big time." The kid would probably be worthless out on the field in this emotional state. If Rick had any hope of turning this game around, he had to get his best running back reoriented, and fast.

"I need you to make it up to me. And the team."

Donnie nodded rapidly, the helmet bobbing. "Anything, Coach."

"You go out there and win that game." He pointed at his chest and poked him. "*You.* You're going to win this game for us. Understand?"

The shifty-eyed panic ebbed away, replaced by concentrated focus. "I understand."

"Make this right, Donnie. Fix it for us."

Donnie squared his shoulders, grim determination settling over his expression like armor. "I'll fix it."

"Yes, you will. Now *go.*" He smacked his ass.

Donnie took off running, looking every inch the star player he was.

Dave had hung back and he fell in beside him now. "Bristol know you're here?"

He shrugged. "I don't give a damn. They can fire me if they want, I'm coaching this team through playoffs."

Dave grinned and thumped him on the back as they stepped out on the field. He drew in a deep breath, the smell of damp grass filling his nostrils. The sight of his kids' new confidence expanded his chest. For the first time on that shit-filled day, something had gone right.

* * *

Brandy saw him on the field a moment before the crowd spotted him. Excitement rippled through the stands. Suddenly everyone was pointing at the tall, broad-shouldered coach, Houston's sweetheart, Rick Morehouse. Her heart fluttered just seeing him back on that field where he belonged. Or was it just seeing him? She missed him, already.

Had Justin been able to fix things? Or had Rick just defied the superintendent and headed down to the field of his own accord?

She looked down the bleachers to where the Justin sat with Dr. Perricone. They had their heads together and Justin was talking. Well, that was what he did best. If ever anyone could win an argument or convince a jury, it was him.

Coral Heights received the second half kickoff and their offense went to work. On first down, their quarterback dropped back to pass but Houston High's d-line penetrated the backfield quickly causing the QB to rush his pass. Straight to Donnie—*yes!* Donnie intercepted the pass! "Yes, Donnie, go! Run!"

Donnie ran, ball tucked up against his chest, weaving and dodging the guys trying to tackle him. He ran the 60 yards and scored.

Yes! The Houston High stands erupted into cheering.

Donnie met his gaze all the way across the field. There was no silly grin or gloating, he just gave him a single nod.

Rick's lips curved into a smile. *Atta boy.* He'd been sure Donnie could turn this game around.

After kicking off, Houston High's defense forced a quick three-and-out and soon their offense was back on the field with the ball.

Sorry suckers.

His boys set up to run a pitch-n-sweep to the right side, and like before, Coral Heights anticipated their moves. But the Houston High QB instead ran a naked bootleg to the left and there was nobody to stop him as he curled around the end and started running.

Tackled on the 30 yard line. Not bad.

He watched the Coral Heights coach scratch his bald head and glanced down at his clipboard, probably wondering if they'd practiced it wrong. Asshole.

The Houston High fans stomped their feet in an organized rhythm, chants growing louder. *Ti-gers, Ti-gers, Ti-gers...*

Houston High set up to run a Power 43 Right Post but the receiver ran a left post instead. Once more, they faked out Coral Heights. Ames completed the pass to Donnie, who had run wide open down the field. He caught it.

The Houston High crowd cheered. No player was even close to Donnie as he booked it down the field, 25 yards and into the end zone.

The crowd screamed. This time Donnie showed a little more pep, holding the ball up in the air in triumph as his teammates slapped him on the back.

They were down 14 to 28. The game was definitely in recovery. He never looked—considered it bad luck, actually—but he turned and gazed up into the stands. As if a homing beacon or a spotlight shone on her, his focus went straight to the tall blonde in the very back. There was no mistaking her elegance and poise.

She smiled broadly, lifting her fingers to wave, then jerking her hand back down and looking around her, as if to be sure he was looking at her.

He resisted the urge to wave back, but his heart seemed to surge back to life, warmth filling his chest. He didn't even remember why he'd been mad at her. It wasn't her fault Stan Brown was a douche.

He dropped his gaze down to the front row, where Bristol and Perricone sat together. Bristol gave him the thumbs up. Huh. Maybe they weren't going to send the cops down on the field to arrest him for being there.

He turned his focus back to the game and clapped his hands. "All right, let's see some good defense now, guys. Show them who's boss."

171

And they did. They tackled the Coral Heights quarterback four times in quick succession, taking the ball back.

The next play showed Coral Heights had given up on following their pilfered playbook, and had finally settled in to just play ball. Fair and square. Too bad they were outclassed by his players. Donnie again streaked down the field and caught the ball, as the third quarter ended.

Still they had one more quarter to go. They would win this game.

* * *

Brandy rubbed her palms on her skinny jeans. She was a sports fan, but not usually the yelling, screaming, sweating it kind. Tonight was different. Somehow, it felt like if Houston High didn't win this game, all her chances of being with Rick were off. Illogical, but there it was.

Claire kicked her feet and looked around, impervious to the fervor of the crowd. All around them, feet were stomping the bleachers, voices were raised to a fever pitch.

Houston High scored their third touchdown and on the ensuing kick-off, the Coral Heights return man fumbled the ball which bounced twice, right into the hands of a Houston High player who ran 10 yards for their fourth touchdown. The cheering crowd was deafening.

Houston High missed the extra point. The score was 27-28 with three minutes left on the clock and Coral Heights had the ball. They called a timeout.

Anyone could predict they'd do their best to run out the clock.

She sat on her hands to keep from chewing her nails, a habit she thought she'd broken years ago. Her mother would be so disappointed in her.

The time out over, the teams came back onto the field.

Come on, come on, come on. They needed a miracle.

Coral Heights ran the ball a few times, getting first downs and burning away precious time on the clock. Coral Heights had pushed the ball past mid-field with 2:38 left on the clock. Not looking good.

Coral Heights ran their next play, but their quarterback fumbled and a scrum ensued to recover the ball. The whistle blew for the two-minute warning as the refs peeled players off the pile to discover Coral Heights retained possession of the ball. Damn.

Please, please, please, God. A miracle. Now.

Coral Heights ran two more running plays as the clock continued to tick down. On third down and long, Coral Heights tried a simple screen pass and-no way— Donnie, the kid Rick had been bringing to the gym, the obvious star of the team, penetrated the line so quickly he was able to tip the ball to himself and intercept it. Again. The kid was incredible. He tucked the ball under his arm and beat a path through the players, ducking and dodging them as they flew at him.

Brandy jumped to her feet, screaming with the rest of the crowd. "Run, Donnie, run!"

He made it! Houston High scored and they won the game!

Everyone jumped up and down and threw their arms around each other. Brandy high-fived Claire and looked around for Sam. With Claire's hand safely tucked in her own, she led her down the bleacher steps, scanning the crowd.

"Daddy!"

Justin pulled Claire in for a hug and kiss. He gave her a nod of his head, like they were spies transmitting secret information.

"Everything's okay?"

"Yeah, it's going to be fine."

She gave him a hug—not a close one, but a hug nonetheless. "Thank you."

He patted her awkwardly. "No problem. Where's Sam?"

At that moment, Sam appeared. "Wasn't that great?" he gushed. "Can you believe that interception?"

"Yeah, they played a great game," Justin said and she stepped back to let them have their moment.

Sam blinked up at his dad. "Why are you here?"

Kids were never subtle.

Justin cocked his head. "I figured I'd better start supporting my son's future team."

Sam's jaw dropped. "Yeah?" A broad grin spread across his face.

Justin dropped a hand on his shoulder. "Yeah. I'm looking forward to watching you play down on that field."

She smiled over the kids' heads at Justin, who matched it.

Wow. She never imagined they'd be on the same side of anything again. It was nice not to have the familiar rancor between them.

Sam's friend from the clinic came up. "Hey, Sam.

The whole team's going to Peter Piper to celebrate. You wanna come?"

Sam looked up at her.

Her chest constricted thinking of Rick. He'd be there. Would he still give her the cold shoulder?

"Yeah, we can go."

"Yes!" He fist pumped the air. "I'll see you there."

"See you there!"

She looked over at Justin. "Do you want to come?"

Please say no.

He shook his head. "Nah. I'll see the kids tomorrow. Have a good time."

"Thanks. For your help, I mean. You were great."

His smile twisted in a wry grin and he shoved his hands in his pockets. "See you guys."

She watched him walk off, a pang of... what? Not regret—she certainly didn't miss her marriage. No, compassion. Yes, that was it. She'd loved him once and she wanted the best for him, even though that wasn't her.

Goodbye, Justin. For the first time since their divorce it felt like a clean break. Like she could go on without hard feelings or the congestion of negativity. Like she could contemplate being in a new relationship...

Chapter Twelve

Rick pulled on his beer. Ted Bristol stood beside him, basking in the glory of his school's championship, making it seem like he'd been Rick's best friend and biggest supporter. Well, whatever, the guy had just been doing his job.

Several more parents pushed their way through to thump him on the back, and Dave handed him another beer. Peter Piper was their default after-game party spot—a kid-friendly restaurant that still had beer and wine for the adults. Priorities.

The kids were all off playing skeeball, chattering excitedly or flirting. Donnie tugged on his sleeve. "Coach, can I talk to you for a second?"

He put his arm around the kid's shoulders and steered him into a corner of the room.

"Coach, are you going to tell everyone?"

He shook his head. "No, I am not. You may choose to tell them on your own, but that's your decision."

"Am I still on the team?" The general rule was if you lost your playbook, you were off the team.

He palmed Donnie's head with both hands. "You think I'm getting rid of you right before State?"

176

Donnie blinked several times, his dark skin reddening. "Is that a no?"

"No. You redeemed yourself, just like I knew you would. And my pal Blake from Texas A&M was there. He told me he'll be paying you a visit tomorrow morning."

Donnie pumped his fist in the air. "Yes! Are you serious? You're not kidding around with me, are you?"

He laughed. "I'm not kidding. Make sure you're up and showered with a shirt and tie when he comes by."

"I will," Donnie said, his eyes darting over toward his mom.

"Go tell her the good news. She'll be proud of you."

"Thanks," he gushed, coming in for a man-hug, thumping Rick on the back.

Rick smiled as he walked jauntily away.

The door swung open and a statuesque blonde walked through it. He wasn't the only one whose head swiveled to take her in. She looked like a model or Hollywood actress—like Christie Brinkley or Paris Hilton.

His heart flip flopped in his chest—unsure of which way to go. Brandy had come.

He hadn't expected her but she'd been on his mind non-stop. He'd been pissed about the article, and he was pretty sure his decision to cool things off with her was right, but he still missed her like a son-of-a-bitch.

And here she was—beautiful. Leggy. Sinfully smart, capable and oh-so-sexy.

Her smile faltered just a little when she saw him, and even though he was still resolved, his chest tightened.

Her kids took off for the games, leaving her unshielded. She drew her shoulders back and lifted her beautiful chin, marching over.

"Congratulations." The air between them rippled with tension.

He honestly wasn't sure how to play this. He settled for "Thanks."

"I know I already texted you, but I'm sorry about the article in *The Chronicle* and the trouble it caused. One of my besties writes for the paper and I had shared how wonderful I think you are."

He might not have believed her, except her cheeks colored slightly when she said it.

"She asked if she could print it and..." she pushed her moon-pale hair from her eyes, "I just didn't think. I didn't see any harm it could do. I made a huge mistake."

He relaxed. She hadn't betrayed him. This was forgivable. But it didn't mean he should open the door back up to their relationship, or anti-relationship, as the case may be. It took great self-control to keep from touching her, but somehow he managed. "No hard feelings. It all worked out. At least I think it did. I haven't heard whether I'll be fired, but considering my principal and super are both here and no one has kicked me out yet, I'm probably okay."

Brandy's eyes turned mournful. "That column was so stupid—"

"Don't give it any more thought. It doesn't deserve it. The Coral Heights players are cheating bastards who will obviously stoop to anything to win. But we just played our best and won."

It all sounded great, so why did he feel so sick? It

was from the hurt he read on Brandy's face. She'd registered his brush-off, the same as she'd noticed it after the first clinic. And it nearly killed him to think he was causing that hurt.

"Well," she said, blinking rapidly. "I'll let you get back to your celebration."

He took another sip of beer to stop himself from wrapping an arm around her waist and telling her she was the only woman for him.

"Thanks." His voice sounded so hollow.

Dr. Perricone interrupted the unhappy scene. "Hello, Brandy." He leaned in to give her a polite cheek kiss.

They knew each other? Oh yeah, her ex had been sitting with him at the game.

"I understand you sent Justin over to give me a little legal counsel on our favorite coach." He thumped Rick on the back while smiling at Brandy.

Rick's skin went cold. What was this?

Brandy appeared pale, her expression frozen in a faint, polite smile. Seeing her like that made his insides churn.

She nodded vaguely. "Well, I wanted he Houston Tigers to win, just like everyone else," she said weakly. "I'm glad he could help. I'm going to, um, get going. Good night to both of you." She turned, making an escape before either of them could answer.

Rick reeled. Had she really sent her ex-husband in to fix things for him? He knew they weren't on great terms, so he doubted that had been an easy favor to ask, especially considering Rick had the impression Justin didn't care about football. At all. He'd be the last person he expected to put himself out for him or the team. Brandy had totally come through for him, unlike Bristol and the board.

And he'd essentially just broken up with her.

Fuck.

* * *

Brandy somehow found her kids and got them out of there. They must've sensed something was wrong with her, because they hardly argued at leaving so soon after arriving.

She just had to hold it together until they went to bed and then she'd have a good cry. She should've followed her better instincts and never succumbed to Rick Morehouse's charming smile. Yes, the sex had been incredible, but it wasn't worth this searing pain, tearing her apart.

She drove home and locked herself in her room, drawing a bath. Her hands shook as she dropped a few drops of lavender oil in the water. Lord knew she needed all the help she could get to relax. She had a feeling she wouldn't be sleeping at all that night.

After stripping, she stepped into the bath and sank all the way down, letting the water cover her face, so only her nose peeked out of the water to breathe. A sob welled up. Tears burned her eyes.

This one night. She'd give herself this one night to grieve Rick Morehouse, and then she'd never think of him again. It had been a mistake. Maybe in time she'd look back on it as a great story. Like, *hey, I had hot monkey sex with the dreamboat Rick Morehouse once. He was a really nice guy.*

She heard her phone ringing in her purse in the

bedroom but she ignored it. She'd bet Angelina or Meg wondered what had happened.

Well, she regretted pissing Rick off, but she wasn't sorry about having the heart to heart with Justin. Having those tensions eased took a big load of stress off her going into the future.

Her stomach twisted. The future. Even though she'd been pretending all along that Rick was only a great lay, some part of her had been planning a future. With him.

Time to let that one go.

* * *

Rick knocked on Brandy's door. It was late. Past midnight. He'd had to stay until the Peter Piper party had ended and all his team had gone home. He'd tried to call ahead to Brandy but she hadn't answered. Lights were on, so she must be home.

No one came to the door.

He knocked again, a little louder.

This was a bad idea. He'd probably scare the hell out of her. No single mom wants to hear a loud knock on her door after midnight.

A change of light behind the peephole told him someone was there.

The door swung open. Brandy stood in a pair of black and pink striped pajamas, looking as drop-dead gorgeous in them as she did in anything. Her brows were drawn together in confused concern. "Rick?"

"Hey," he murmured, keeping his voice low to not wake her kids. "May I come in?"

She didn't move aside. "It's kind of late."

He stabbed his fingers through his hair. "I know. I'm sorry. I tried to call. I wanted to apologize."

He needed to apologize for doubting her. To tell her he wanted more. He wanted all of her. Would she go for it, though?

She just might. He knew she cared. She wouldn't have worked so hard to help him out if she didn't. But he'd hurt her.

She still didn't move to let him in. "The kids are asleep and I'm exhausted."

Okay, he could work with a talk on her doorstep.

"I just wanted to thank you for getting your ex to talk to Perricone."

She flushed, her pale skin glowing under the porch light. "It's the least I could do."

"No." He shook his head. "This wasn't your fault. At first I thought you might have been using me for publicity for your gym, but now I realized I had my head wedged. You're not like that. I misjudged the situation and gave you the cold shoulder. I apologize."

Her eyes glittered with unshed tears. She didn't speak. He suspected she didn't trust her voice to be steady.

"I hurt you and I'm truly sorry."

She shrugged, looking away. Forgiveness, but no engagement.

"There's something else…" He drew a breath, searching for the right words. "I missed you, Brandy." He waved a hand, "I mean, I know it's only been a few days, but when I was thinking about us not seeing each other anymore, it… it bothered me so much more than I expected." He gave her a rueful look. "You're under my skin, Brandy Love."

The corners of her mouth lifted. It wasn't a full smile, but it did seem genuine. "I missed you, too."

He wanted to kiss her right there—to re-assert his interest, but he didn't want to push yet. Standing with her in the doorway and him outside was a metaphor he needed to change. "Come here, I need to show you something." He grabbed her hand and tugged her out onto the porch with him. Maybe before they had the big "talk" about moving their relationship forward, they should reconnect in the way that already had been working—with passion.

She laughed. "What are you showing me?"

He steered her down the steps and along the sidewalk to his car. "I want to show you my trophy," he said in a suggestive voice. He pushed her up against the Escalade and pressed his body against hers.

She stiffened and he almost pulled back, but then she melted into him. "Rick..." Her voice was half amusement, half reproach.

He cupped her head and lowered his mouth to hers, claiming it without preamble or warning.

She responded, softening into him, pressing her lips back against his. Her slender hands slid up to his chest, remaining there. He threaded his fingers through her silky blonde hair. "I need you."

That was the God's honest truth.

If ever a man needed sexual healing, it was him. His day had been a nightmare and all he wanted was to forget it in the taste of her.

"Rick... my kids."

"I know. I'm not asking. Just wishing." He gave her a rueful smile. "I'm serious when I say I need you."

"Tomorrow's Saturday."

He inhaled her scent, nuzzled her neck. "I'd like to take you on a date. To talk about our no dating policy."

Her eyes crinkled with amusement. "Well... I might be able to bend my personal rule just this once."

"Good." He kissed her again. "I'll pick you up at the gym." He eased back, freeing her.

Her breath seemed unsteady, her eyes dilated. A strand of her cornsilk hair fell across her eyes.

He brushed it back, touching her cheek with the backs of his knuckles.

"You gonna show me that trophy?" she challenged. He loved the flirty tone.

"Mmm hmm. And more." He wanted something way beyond their sex-at-the-gym game this time, though. "It will be a proper date."

His phone buzzed and he pulled it out. A text from Phil had come through, *8 lbs, 2 oz healthy baby girl. Amy's fine.*

"Yes!" He pumped his fist in the air. Quite the turnaround this day.

"What?" Brandy asked.

"My buddy Phil just had a baby girl. He had to leave in the middle of the game." He kissed her again. "You'll meet them soon."

It was a promise. He wanted his life intersected with hers. Forever.

Chapter Thirteen

She hadn't been this nervous for a date since high school. It was silly because her comfort level with Rick surpassed any other "date." Still, her expectations for this one were sky high.

She showered at the club and put on her sexiest dress—a turquoise and dark blue patterned affair that showed off her curves, clinging to her breasts and hips and accentuating her narrow waist. Remembering how much he'd enjoyed them last time, she donned a pair of navy thigh highs and her dressiest cowgirl boots— the soft brown ones with turquoise stitching.

As she blew her hair dry, she almost laughed at the nervous flutters in her belly. Forty-four years old and a man could still give her jitters.

But he wasn't any man. Rich Morehouse was more than she'd ever dreamed he'd be. And they had a lot to discuss. She could only interpret his request for a talk about their "no dating" rules as a desire to change the status quo. Because if he wanted to end things, he wouldn't have shown up at her house the night before to apologize.

One of her regular customers walked into the ladies locker room and smiled. "You must have a date."

"I sure do."

185

With Houston's sweetheart, no less.

"Are you waiting for me to get out of here? All I have to do is grab my stuff and go."

"Take your time, I don't even know if he's here yet."

But he was. She found him leaning against the front desk looking... drool-worthy. Dead sexy with his boyish smile lighting up his face.

He straightened up and his smile widened as his eyes traveled down to her boots and back up again, lingering on her face. "Hello, gorgeous." He looked clean-shaven and fresh, his button-down shirt and slacks pressed.

Good, they were on the same wavelength as far as dressing for the date.

"Hey, handsome."

He snaked an arm around her waist and pulled her against his body, stealing a kiss. "You look beautiful."

She touched his collar. "So do you."

"How many people do I need to kick out before we can leave?"

She laughed. "Are you going to kick them out?"

"Yep. I'm going to tell them they're standing between me and a hot date, and they'd better get a move on, if they know what's good for them."

"It's been slow this week because of Christmas. There's only one in the ladies locker room. Why don't you check the men's?"

"You bet. I'll be right back."

He strode through the gym, flicking off lights, as if he worked there. He was so damn competent. The client from the ladies' room came out and winked. "Have a great time on your date."

"Thanks, you too. I mean have a good night!"

186

Lordy, was she blushing? Rick seemed to have that effect on her.

Rick reappeared. "We're all clear."

She pulled out her keys. "Great, let's go."

He took the keys from her and held the door open, then locked it after them.

She could get used to having someone take care of these little things.

"You're coming in my car," Rick murmured, propelling her toward his Escalade. She didn't mind letting him drive this time. In fact, it was easy to let a man lead when he was just as willing to follow. Rick Morehouse was like no other man she'd ever known, that was for sure.

He drove to Diva, the fancy bar and restaurant attached to the Westingford Resort. Inside, they found a cozy booth in the bar/lounge, sipping cocktails and listening to the live Latin music. She sat close to him, her body tingling every place they touched. Frissons of heat rippled through her every time she looked into his jade green eyes and her clit pulsed in anticipation of their future recreation.

"I wanted to thank you again for getting your ex to advise the superintendent. Apparently that's the reason I still have a job." He picked up her hand, rubbing his thumb across her pulse.

"Yeah, I sort of hated cashing in that favor, but it actually worked out for the best. I finally pulled on my big girl panties and owned up to my half of the relationship fail."

Rick's gaze burned into her. She worried for a moment it was inappropriate to talk about Justin. But Rick had brought him up. He stroked his fingertips down each of her fingers. "It takes emotional maturity to view a failed relationship that way. Most people never get there."

She swallowed, his praise meaning more to her than it should.

"Yeah, I honestly could've gone on for years with the stiff, contentious way of relating we've had. But then I couldn't beg him for a favor." She smiled ruefully. "So I did what I should've done the day after we divorced—I forgave him."

Some kind of pain rippled across Rick's face and she worried again about the topic.

"I should probably take a page from your book. My dad showed up at my door yesterday to tell me he's dying." Rick's expression twisted with emotion. "How do I even take that? On one hand, I don't even know the guy. We have no relationship. On the other... he's my *father*."

She squeezed his palm. "God, that's so hard. I'm so sorry."

"Yeah, I froze up. I just sort of... sent him away."

"Well, what do you want from the situation?"

The pain in Rick's eyes tore her apart. He rubbed his jaw. "I don't want a relationship. But I don't want to turn my back on him, either."

"Of course not. You can treat him with compassion without giving the message that you approve of the way he acted in the past. I believe sometimes, that's why we resist forgiving. We think it let's the other person off the hook. But it reality, it just let's us off the hook."

Rick's nostrils flared and he drew a deep breath. "Maybe you're right." His voice sounded strangled.

"Maybe... you can help me through this. You seem pretty wise."

Her heart skittered. That wasn't the kind of thing one said to just a fuck-buddy.

* * *

"So about dating..." Rick lost his breath looking into the clear blue depths of Brandy's eyes. "I propose a re-evaluation of our present stance on a relationship."

She regarded him without speaking.

What was going on in that beautiful head of hers? His blunt-cut nails dug into his palms.

"I want to date you, Brandy. I want more than sex. I really care about you."

Her throat worked. "What about..." She swallowed. "What about the kids?"

"I love your kids," he said without the slightest hesitation. "And I definitely don't want to hurt them. But that's not going to happen. I'm going in with the intention of playing for keeps, Brandy. Are you in?"

She blinked rapidly.

He held his breath.

Her head wobbled.

Was it a yes? No... her head moved in a circle. Was that a no? He cocked his head to the side, trying to decipher her non-answer.

He picked up her hand and brought her fingers to his lips. "This is where you're supposed to shout, "Yes, Coach Morehouse.""

She smiled. "Yes, Coach Morehouse." It was a whisper, not a shout, but it was good enough for him. He stood up and tugged her to stand.

He had booked a room at the resort for the night and he couldn't wait to get Brandy naked. And it wasn't just for the sex. He wanted to show her what she meant to him, how much he needed her in his life.

"Are you ready to go?" Brandy looked surprised as she pulled her purse onto her shoulder.

"Yes." He stood up and offered his hand. "I can't wait another minute to be with you."

Her blue eyes darkened. "It's going to be a long drive home," she said in her husky sex voice.

"We're not leaving." He pulled the resort keycard from his pocket and flashed it at her.

Her eyes widened, lips curving into a sultry smile. "I like the way you think, Coach."

Somehow, he made it into the elevator without pawing her, but the moment the doors closed, he had her up against the wall, hands filled with her curves as he nibbled the length of the side of her neck.

Her gasp made his cock go rock hard, her vanilla scent made him want to devour her. He couldn't wait to worship between her legs.

The doors slid open and he swung her, giggling, up into his arms and carried her down the hall. She took the key card and opened the door with it, and he stepped across the threshold.

"This means you're mine now," he said.

"Oh really?" A touch of feminist disbelief rang in her voice.

He chuckled. "That's right. I'm laying claim to you. I've carried you over the threshold, that means I get to keep you." He tossed her on the bed, and yanked off her cowgirl boots.

"Is that some kind of pirate law or something?"

"Coach's law. You haven't heard of it? I was in possession of the female when I crossed the threshold to a bedroom. That means I get to keep her."

She snorted, but helped him by peeling off her panties.

He crawled over her, shoving her skirt up to her waist and shimmying it off her shoulders and head.

Her blue lacy bra matched her panties and the thigh-highs. His brain galloped off wondering how many more sexy ensembles she owned and crashed when he wondered who else had seen them.

Mine. Some Neanderthal part of his brain beat its chest. He needed her to be his and only his. Forever.

He'd make Brandy Love ache for him until she agreed to those terms. He gripped her thighs and parted them.

Oh, holy mother of God. He drank in the sight of Brandy's beautiful pussy. The neatly trimmed landing strip of hair, the rest shaven bare. Her lips were plump and dew glistened at the slit.

His breath grew short, cock throbbed. "You have a porn pussy, Brandy Love." His voice sounded strangled.

She laughed her husky laugh, a blush tinging her cheeks. He loved it when she blushed.

He pushed her knees back toward her shoulders and licked along the seam of her pussy, parting her lips with his tongue and tracing all the delicate parts.

She gasped, rolling her hips up to meet him. He sucked a lip.

"*Rick!* Oh God..." She grasped his head, threading her fingers into his hair.

He heard the urgency already ringing in her

voice. The same driving need burned in him but, he planned to take his time tonight. To bring her right up to the edge and leave her there until she begged for it.

He flicked his tongue over her clit, then returned to teasing her lips, licking and sucking at a leisurely place, even though his thighs tensed and his hands shook with lust.

"Rick... oh *please.* It's too much... too much. You're driving me mad."

He lifted his head to look at his beautiful woman splayed out on the bed, her pale blonde hair fanned out and glowing against the bedspread. She arched, thrusting her satin and lace-encased breasts toward the ceiling.

He brought his thumb to her clit and drew a slow circle around it.

"Yes," she choked.

He settled back to his haunches and resumed his tongue torture, flicking and sucking at her labia, making his tongue stiff and penetrating her with it.

"Inside me," she panted. "Please. I need you inside me."

His cock jerked, and he groaned. She was killing him.

"This pussy," he said, screwing two fingers inside her, "Is mine. Only mine." He stroked her inner wall and she screamed, writhing beneath his fingers. He pumped them in and out. "No more elicit booty-calls, no more Saturday night workouts at the gym. I need more of you. All of you."

"*God, Rick!*" She came, her internal muscles squeezing his fingers, clamping down as she thrust her hips up to meet him.

He pumped his fingers in and out three times and thrust them deep, keeping them there until her climax finished. After easing them out, he climbed over her. "Did you hear me? I want you exclusively. You and everything that comes with you. The whole package—kids, business, a car that needs repairs, even if you're too stubborn to let me help. Whatever you got, I want to be a part of it."

She stared up at him as if he'd lost his mind.

"I know this is fast. I know I did a 180. But yesterday my world turned on its head, and even though I pushed you away, you were still a rock, right there with me. And in the end, when I was down there on that field, I had it in my mind that I had to live up to your expectations. Because you must've said some pretty nice things for your friend to write that article about me."

Her face had gone soft, her gaze loving. She reached up to touch his face. "Yeah, I guess I feel the same. I was pushing this thing away, but as soon as I thought it was lost, my world fell apart too."

He crushed his lips to hers, covering her body with his own, drinking in her soft warmth. Her arms twined around his neck and she kissed him back with a fervor he hadn't felt from her before. He rocked the bulge of his clothed cock into her moist heat, groaning into her mouth.

She slid her hands down his sides and fumbled with the button on his slacks.

He took charge, pushing himself off her to quickly strip and don a condom.

Heat blazed in her eyes as she watched him crawl back over her. He nibbled her ear and neck, then rolled

193

her over to her belly and lifted her hips, so she came up to her knees, her chest still resting on the bed.

He stroked his palm down the long, graceful arch of her back.

She wiggled her hips in a beautiful invitation.

Unable to resist one second longer, he impaled her with his cock. The shout from his lips filled the room as he sank into her tight, wet heat. She squeezed his length with her internal muscles, her body control outstanding.

He couldn't wait—couldn't go slow or be gentle. He thrust into her hard, gripping her hips to hold her steady. "Brandy..." he groaned. It was his form of an apology. He teetered on the edge of control.

"Yes," she wailed.

"Yes?"

His vision had tunneled. He wanted to slow down, to make sure she climaxed again, but his hips thrust of their own accord, punishing her with his need, his burning desire.

"*Yes.*" Her throaty gasp sent him over the edge. He fucked her even harder, blood rushing from his brain straight to his cock. His balls tensed.

He reached around the front of her hips and rubbed her clit at the same moment he shoved in so deep he pushed her off her knees and onto her belly.

She bowed up, legs lifting behind them, taut and shaking, a hoarse scream coming from her mouth.

He thought he'd never stop coming. Stars danced before his eyes as he shot his load, filling the condom, already wishing for their future, when they might have sex without one.

He collapsed on top of her, rolling them both to

the side to keep from crushing her with his weight. His arm curved around her flat belly and he stroked it lightly, then wandered lower, between her legs to tap her clit once more.

She spasmed again, a tiny ripple of after-orgasm shuddering through her. "Wow," she murmured.

"Sorry, I couldn't hold back. Was I too rough?"

"You were amazing." Her voice had a dreamy quality.

He nuzzled his face into her silky hair.

"So you're really okay with my kids?"

"I want to be in your life. I also want to protect your kids from getting hurt, but I've come to the conclusion that there are no guarantees in life. I can't promise things will work out, but I sure want to give it a try."

"I have parents, too," she said, a testing quality.

He chuckled. "I can do other people's parents, just not my dad."

"My dad had a stroke two years ago. He's a huge fan of yours. I'd love for him to meet you."

"Yes. He's going to meet me. I'm the man you're dating, remember?" It was his winning coach stubbornness rearing its head, pushing her when he probably should let her breathe. He needed to seal this deal, right here, right now. He wanted this game—the one that felt more important than any championship he'd ever coached or played—in the bag.

Brandy rolled over to face him. "You're really serious about this? About a relationship?"

He brushed a strand of her moonbeam hair out of her face. "Dead serious."

Her lips curved into a teasing grin. "Serious enough to meet my parents?"

"I would be honored."

"Do you think your dad would like to come to the Fostering Christmas party tomorrow night?"

"My dad?" He tried not to choke. Thinking of his dad taking any part in his life still made his brain stutter to a stop.

"Sure. Why not invite him? He may not feel up to it, but at least you're opening a door. And it's a low-risk way to see him. He's not going to fight the kids for time with Santa."

For the first time the constriction in his chest that was always there when he thought about his father eased slightly. Brandy would know how to manage him. They'd figure things out.

Together.

Chapter Fourteen

Brandy watched Meg bustle around, adjusting food trays and napkins on the linen-covered tables against the wall. Both her kids and Meg's helped out, following Meg's flurry of directions for setup.

Gleaming silver carafes of hot apple cider and hot cocoa stood on one end, beside the eggnog chilling in an ice bucket. Trays upon trays of kid-friendly finger foods, ranging from savory to sweet lined the rest of the table.

Meg had done a bang-up job getting the Fostering Christmas party thrown together with almost no time to plan. They'd set up in Studio A, one of her largest rooms and Meg had put up a cheerful Christmas tree, trimmed in all edibles so the kids could take the treats off and eat them. Candy canes and red and green popcorn balls hung from the branches. Under the tree were the piles of small stocking-style gifts, all wrapped and separated into bins according to age and gender.

Rick was back in the men's locker room, putting on his Santa suit. He would bring in two large sacks full of wrapped gifts with the foster children's names on them.

The press, sponsors and large donors would be here any minute, then the foster families would arrive.

Meg hurried over, her black heels clicking on the hardwood floor. "How does everything look?"

"Amazing. Really. I'm so glad you took on this project. I would've just thrown out some cookies and punch and been done with it."

Angelina and Juliet came in together, all dressed festively. Angelina wore a large camera around her neck.

"You *came*," Meg bustled over to them like the perfect hostess. It was nice to have someone else sharing the responsibility for a change.

"We wouldn't miss it for the world. You're first big event," Juliet said. "And I'm here to cover it for *Houston Magazine*," Angelina said.

"Oh," Meg fumbled with her purse. "I had cards made, do you want to see?"

"Ooh, yes."

"Meg's Parties & More," she chirped, handing them each a floral print card.

"What's the *and more*?" Juliet asked.

Meg shrugged. "Ah don't *know*," her southern accent made her sound ditzier than she was. Or else she played that card as a learned habit. They all knew she was anything but. The poor woman had been a genius with no one to appreciate her talents except her growing kids and often absent husband. "It leaves it open for possibility," she winked, her smile slightly naughty.

Brandy loved seeing her all lit up like this.

"You two stand together, I definitely need a photo of Houston's most successful female entrepreneurs."

Angelina shooed them together and snapped several pictures.

A television camera and crew moved in from the local Channel Four news. "This is a perfect human interest story for the holiday," the reporter said when Brandy thanked them for coming. "We'll just get set up in the back, here."

"Perfect, thank you."

The Child and Family Center social worker poked her head in. "The foster families should be here in about 45 minutes."

Brandy looked at her watch, surprised. "I thought they were coming at 6:00?"

The social worker's brow furrowed. "I told them all 6:30. I'm sorry—I might have screwed that up."

"No problem. I'd better go tell Santa he can relax, then." She smiled and excused herself, letting Meg know the change in schedule before heading down to give Rick the news. The poor guy had been holed up in the men's locker room for 30 minutes already.

With a light tap on the locker room door, she pushed it open.

Rick had his hat and beard off, and his boyish grin swindled her breath. "Ready for me?" He'd already made his voice sound jolly.

She giggled. "There's been a slight delay, Santa. The kids won't be here for 45 more minutes."

He rolled his eyes. "Ugh. Really?"

"I'm sorry, can I bring you a book or a magazine?"

His eyelids lowered. "You could stay back here and entertain me. This is sort of... *our place.*"

She snorted. "The men's locker room is not *our place!*"

He laughed. "What? Not romantic enough?" He made a show of looking around the room. "I don't know, I find it pretty seductive."

She ought to be out there helping Meg get things in order. But then, that's why she'd hired Meg, wasn't it? To handle the event for her?

Rick must have sensed her resolve crumbling because he smirked and put on the mustache-beard combo and the Santa-hat, and sauntered toward her. He crushed her against the closed door, kissing her. "Have you been a good girl, Brandy?"

She bit her lip and shook her head, slowly, making her eyes wide like an ingénue. "No, Santa. I've been very naughty."

His green eyes twinkled. "Mmm," he rumbled and kissed her again. "Santa likes naughty girls."

"He does?" she giggled again. "Do you have the wrong script?"

He grinned. "Only because he gets to spank them," he whispered.

She looked at her watch. "We do have a little time... "

Rick's eyes darkened. He reached behind her to turn the lock on the door, then claimed her hand and tugged her away from the door. "Come on, little girl, let's go check my list to see what you're getting for Christmas."

She found herself bent over the countertop, her lustful reflection staring back at her as Santa slid the hem of her dress up over her waist.

He peeled her panties down and ran his large, calloused palm over her sensitized skin. "Mmm, yes, this is a naughty little ass."

She shivered, anticipation shooting through her, her pussy growing moist. "Santa, is this what you always do to naughty girls?"

"Only the most deserving." He brought his palm down on one of her cheeks.

Would they hear out there in the studio? Surely not, but the thrill of knowing all the press, donors and family were right there while she was getting naughty with Santa only amplified her desire. She bit her lip.

He rubbed away the sting before leaving a handprint on the other side.

Her pussy clenched. "Rick…"

He slapped her harder, twice. "That's Santa to you, young lady."

She giggled. "Oops, I meant Santa."

He brushed a finger across her wet folds. "Yes?"

She gasped as he flicked her clit. "I-I think you'd better get on with it. Not to rush you or anything, but I probably can't be gone too long." He breached her entrance with one finger.

He made a tsking sound. "Can't make time for Santa, huh? Well, all right, but I'm not sure how well Santa can drill you with this big stuffed belly in the way."

She met his laughing eyes in the mirror and broke down into a fit of giggles.

He lifted the stuffed belly up and shoved it to the side. "What? This isn't sexy to you?" He fumbled with a condom before shoving his pants down.

"Santa, you're always sexy to me… ung, yes," she groaned as Rick pushed into her. She hardly needed foreplay with him, the mere sight of him had her panties damp and her pussy raring to go. The big stuffed belly bopped on her hip as he eased in and out, holding her gaze in the mirror.

"Santa…," she panted.

He chuckled and picked up his speed. "Hush, naughty girl. And no screaming this time, we don't want to disturb the children."

She pushed her hips back at him, laughing. With her hands braced against the countertop, she held firm for his in strokes, squeezed his cock with her internal muscles. Thank God for Kegels, they made sex so much better…

Rick bent his knees, changing the angle of his thrusts and she came unglued.

Pressing her lips together to keep her scream in, she made a strangled sound.

"Yes," he hissed.

"Yes."

"Yes, God *yes*." He plunged deep inside her and stayed there.

She climaxed, too, clamping down on his cock with her muscles, moaning through pinched lips.

He eased out and disposed of the condom, righting his costume.

She cleaned herself and pulled up her panties. "I can't believe I just got naughty with Santa."

Rick pulled his cottony beard aside and kissed her, trailing a fingertip up her arm. "Santa doesn't find you naughty at all. He thinks you're very, very good."

She leaned into his cushioned belly and smiled up at him. "I'll go check on things. The kids should be arriving in the next 20 minutes."

Rick winked. "I'll be ready."

* * *

Rick tossed the bags of toys over his shoulder and shouted, "Ho, ho, ho," as he headed down the hallway.

The studio was packed with children of all ethnicities and ages and the festive Christmas anticipation pulsed in the air. The smaller children grew excited, rising to their knees, eyes shining. Older ones rolled their eyes or scoffed, but they still eyed the sacks with interest.

He'd helped Meg and Brandy and their kids wrap all the gifts that morning. The social worker had provided them with a list of names and ages and they'd matched them with donations. Not much had come in for the older kids, but they'd had monetary donations, which Brandy used to buy presents. Good ones, too. She'd brought her kids to help pick them out.

He plopped down in the chair designated for "Santa" and started pulling out the gifts and reading the nametags. The children ran forward to collect their gifts. It seemed like it took forever, but probably went pretty fast.

He was down to just a few gifts when he pulled out one and blinked at the name.

"Who is it for?" a child in the front asked.

He cleared his throat. "Darrell Morehouse?"

The kids all sat still. Movement in the back of the room drew his attention. His father had been sitting down in the far corner. He shuffled forward now.

Brandy had done this. That sweet little vixen.

He stood up and threaded his way through the children to hand the gift to his father. "You must've been very good this year," he said. "You're the only adult who's been given a gift!"

The adults in the room chuckled. His father's eyes watered as he took the gift with a shaking hand. "Thank you." His voice sounded thin. Old.

"I'm glad you could be here," he said in a low tone.

His father bobbed his head, seeming too emotional to speak. He clutched the gift to his torso like a football as he shuffled back to his seat.

A smile tugging at his lips, he looked over at Brandy, who flashed her brilliant smile back. She might need another spanking from Santa before he was through.

Heart warm, he sat back down and finished the gift giving. The children, who hadn't bothered to wait to open gifts, now got up and crowded around the food tables for refreshments, leaving a massive pile of wrapping paper and ribbon on the rug.

Brandy's friend Meg rushed in, directing Brandy's employee Jennie to bring another garbage bag to collect it all.

Before he took his place by the door to hug the children as they left, he sat back in his chair and watched it all, the din of chattering children, the cheerful voices, his father opening his gift in the corner. This was the sort of life he'd always wanted. A full one—with lots of people to love and a beautiful woman beside him to share it all.

* * *

Brandy sighed, happy but exhausted. The children and their families had left, as had most of the press.

"Santa" had gone over to talk to his dad, and everything seemed okay there.

"Well, great job, lady," Juliet said, sidling up to her.

"Yeah," she sighed. "I think it went well."

"It was fabulous." Angelina joined them.

"And what a hunky Santa," Meg teased, lifting her chin toward Rick, who had sat back down on his Santa's chair while several photographers snapped his photo. He'd been posing all night, infinitely patient with the attention from both the press and fans. "The press showed up just to see him, you know."

"Totally, that's why I asked him." The photographers finished and moved away.

"Do I get to sit on Santa's lap?" Juliet teased, pretending to run over to him, while grinning broadly at Brandy.

Brandy took the bait, racing her to throw herself on Rick's lap.

He caught her, laughing and wrapping his arms around her.

She tugged his beard down and kissed him, only to see flashbulb going off. She spun around, ready to tell the person off, but it was Angelina.

"I'm going to call this one... Naughty Moments with Santa," she said, grinning. "May I print it? Pretty please?"

She looked at Rick, whose eyes crinkled. "I'd be honored to be featured in a picture with the owner of Phenomenal Physiques."

She elbowed him in the ribs, laughing. "Okay by me. But I'm sure Stan Brown will start saying that we're running a child slave trade from China or something."

For a moment she worried it was too soon to joke,

205

but everyone laughed and Rick's arms tightened around her.

His father shuffled over and they both stood up. "Well, Rick, are you going to introduce me to your girlfriend?" he rasped.

To her satisfaction, Rick didn't flinch. "This beautiful lady is Brandy Love, the owner of Phenomenal Physiques and the woman I hope to marry someday, once I convince her."

Brandy's friends gasped, and gave her illicit thumbs' up signals. Sam and Claire, who'd been hanging out with Meg's kids watched with curiosity.

She extended her palm and shook Rick's father's hand.

"I'm Darrell," he said.

"Nice to meet you."

She noticed he didn't lay claim to being Rick's father, nor had Rick claimed him, but they were interacting. It was a start.

"Darrell, would you like to join us for Christmas dinner at my parents? Rick will be there." She darted a glance at Rick, hoping he wouldn't kill her. It was presumptuous of her and she wished she'd had a chance to ask him what he thought before she'd spoken.

Rick didn't look upset, though. His eyes shone with appreciation.

The old man beamed. "Thank you, I'd like that."

She smiled back. "Great, then it's settled."

Rick wrapped an arm around her waist and squeezed her against him. She sensed his appreciation pouring into her from the places their bodies connected. She fit there, nestled against his side. It seemed easy and comfortable, as if they'd always been together.

Epilogue

Rick and his father arrived at Brandy's parents for Christmas dinner. He'd spent the morning with his mother, but she had been invited to dinner with friends, so he'd left guilt-free. She had, however, insisted on meeting Brandy and her kids as soon as possible.

He shifted the giant box of presents he'd brought to tap on the door. Claire pulled the door open, her angelic smile full of Christmas excitement. "Rick!"

He loved her warm greeting. "Hi Claire." He stepped in. "Did you meet my father, Darrell, at the Fostering Christmas event?"

Claire eyed his dad curiously and shook her head. "No."

His dad stuck out his hand. "Hi there, young lady. I'm Darrell."

Sam rounded the corner, followed by Brandy and a white-haired older version of Brandy.

Brandy rushed forward to take the gifts from him. "Please come in. This is my mom, Sylvia."

He shook her hand. Her blue eyes were as sharp as Brandy's, the intelligence beneath them just as bright. "Coach Morehouse, thank you for coming."

"It's my pleasure."

Brandy returned from depositing the presents, greeted his father with a kiss and hooked her hand in his elbow. "Come and meet my dad." She beckoned to his father. "You, too, Darrell. Please come in."

She led him to the living room, which was decked out with a tree in one corner, piled high with presents. A balding man sat in a recliner, his head turned in the direction of their entrance.

"Daddy, Coach Morehouse is here," Brandy said brightly.

Although he didn't speak, his face took on a look of exaggerated surprise and delight. He held out a trembling hand, seeming to work hard to unclench his fingers before they pressed palms.

He made sure to look him right in the eye and squeeze firmly. "Mr. Love, it's a pleasure to meet you. I'm a big fan of your daughter."

"It's George," Sylvia corrected him. "He's a huge fan of yours. Always has been, and even more so since you started coaching high school. George was a lifelong educator and a high school principal." The pride in her voice stirred him.

Her dad pointed a finger from him to Brandy and back again, a question forming on his face. "Yoooou?"

Brandy slid up right beside him, slipping her hand through his elbow again. "Yes, Daddy. I'm seeing Rick."

Shocked pleasure registered on his face.

Brandy rolled her eyes. "I told him that before, but I guess he didn't believe me." There was an affectionate, teasing quality to her voice.

The Loves lived up to their name—there was no

shortage of attachment here. It stood out in stark contrast to his own relationship with his father, but this time, rather than pain him, he felt hope. Like, with Brandy at his side, he might untangle the threads that held him prisoner, and find some resolution. Hopefully before his father died.

He looked over at his dad, who hung back, in the doorway and beckoned him in. "George and Sylvia, this is my dad, Darrell Morehouse. He's just moved back to Houston this month." He left out the *to die* part.

"Well, who wants to open their presents?" Rick chortled, returning to his role of Santa Claus.

"I do, I do," the two kids sang out.

Everyone sat down and the kids passed out gifts.

"They've already opened gifts at their father's this morning," Brandy laughed. She looked happy, her face relaxed, her smile easy.

He winked at her.

She beamed back.

All these years he'd never known what he'd been missing. This. A big family. Kids. A strong, beautiful woman. He wanted to ask her to marry him already, but knew it was too soon. He'd need to court the kids first, and her parents. But by next year, he resolved, Brandy would be his, forever.

About the Authors

USA Today Bestselling Author **Renee Rose** loves a dominant, dirty-talking alpha hero! Readers have devoured over five million copies of her steamy romance with varying levels of kink. Her books have been featured in *USA Today*'s Happily Ever After and Popsugar. Named Eroticon USA's Next Top Erotic Author in 2013, she's gone on to hit the *USA Today* list 15 times with her Chicago Bratva, Bad Boy Alpha, Wolf Ranch books, and various anthologies.

Theresa Roemer is an author, media personality, entrepreneur and small business owner based in Houston, Texas.

Theresa's passion for health started at a young age. As a child Theresa was diagnosed with rheumatic fever many times over, which caused her to have a heart murmur; she was sickly and her doctors diagnosed her with a lifetime of physical constraints. Determined to prove the doctors wrong, Theresa began her lifelong journey to stay active, healthy, and physically fit. Theresa took the U.S. Open title in bodybuilding at the age of 40, and held the titles of Mrs. Houston U.A., Mrs. Texas U.A., and was the 1st runner up for Mrs. United America concurrently.

Theresa's passion for health inspired her to write Naked in 30 Days to empower women to feel as vibrant and healthy at 45 and beyond as they did at 25. This is her first work of fiction.

Visit Theresa on www.theresaroemer.com, Instagram Theresa_Roemer, Facebook Theresa Roemer LLC and X @TheresaRoemer

Other Riverdale Avenue Books You Might Enjoy

Naked in 30 Days:
A One-Month Guide to Getting Your Body, Mind and Spirit in Shape
By Theresa Roemer

A Scarlet Christmas
By DL King

Her Stepbrother's Christmas Gift:
A Once Upon a Stepbrother Novella
By Rachel Kenley

Whips and Chains and Candy Canes
By Faith Bicknell Brown

Wrapped Around Your Handlebars
By Ana Lee Kennedy

Holiday Smut
Edited by Lori Perkins

Home Alone for Christmas
By Lori Perkins

Bad Santa
By Lise Horton

Capricorn: Cursed
Book One of the Witch Upon a Star Series
By Sephera Giron

Not Home for the Holiday
By Isabelle Drake

Jingle Balls: A Christmas Anthology
Edited by Cecilia Tan and Isabella Flynn

A Christmas Carl: A Gay Retelling of A Christmas
Carol
By Ryan Field

Christmas Magic
By Cecilia Tan

Holiday Gay
Edited by Maitland McDonough

Happy Holigays
By Matthew Cooper